YEARLING

D0361546

‹018

Since 1966, Yearling has been the

leading name in classic and award-winning

literature for young readers.

With a wide variety of titles,

Yearling paperbacks entertain, inspire,

and encourage a love of reading.

VISIT

WWW.RANDOMHOUSE.COM/KIDS

**TO FIND THE PERFECT BOOK, PLAY GAMES,
AND MEET FAVORITE AUTHORS!**

OTHER YEARLING BOOKS YOU WILL ENJOY

ALViN HO

ALLErGIC TO CAMPING, HIKING, AND OTHEr NATURAL DISASTErS

BY **Lenore LOOk** PICTUREs BY LeUyen Pham

A YEARLING BOOK

Text copyright © 2009 by Lenore Look
Illustrations copyright © 2009 by LeUyen Pham

All rights reserved. Published in the United States by Yearling, an imprint of Random House Children's Books, a division of Random House, Inc., New York. Originally published in hardcover in the United States by Schwartz & Wade Books, an imprint of Random House Children's Books, a division of Random House, Inc., New York, in 2009.

Yearling and the jumping horse design are registered trademarks of Random House, Inc.

Visit us on the Web! www.randomhouse.com/kids

Educators and librarians, for a variety of teaching tools, visit us at
www.randomhouse.com/teachers

The Library of Congress has cataloged the hardcover edition of this work as follows:
Look, Lenore.
Alvin Ho : allergic to camping, hiking, and other natural disasters / Lenore Look ;
illustrated by LeUyen Pham.
p. cm.
Summary: When Alvin's father takes him camping to instill a love of nature,
like that of their home-town hero Henry David Thoreau, Alvin makes a new friend
and learns that he can be brave despite his fear of everything.
ISBN 978-0-375-85705-8 (trade) — ISBN 978-0-375-95705-5 (Gibraltar lib. bdg.) —
ISBN 978-0-375-85393-7 (e-book)
[1. Camping—Fiction. 2. Fear—Fiction. 3. Self-confidence—Fiction.
4. Friendship—Fiction. 5. Chinese Americans—Fiction. 6. Concord (Mass.)—Fiction.]
I. Pham, LeUyen, ill. II. Title.
PZ7.L8682Akt 2009
[F]—dc22
2008045845

ISBN 978-0-375-85750-8 (pbk.)

Printed in the United States of America

20 19 18 17 16 15 14

First Yearling Edition

This book belongs to
Francisco Nahoe,
Who has helped Alvin out of the woods
More than once.
—L.L.

To Atticus, who wanted another Alvin Ho book—
this one is for you!
—L.P.

AUTHOR'S ACKNOWLEDGMENTS

It is a common accident for men camping in the woods to be
killed by a falling tree.
   —Henry David Thoreau, "The Allegash and East Branch,"
   The Maine Woods, 1864

With many thanks to:
Ann Kelley, for being infinitely patient and long-suffering.

LeUyen Pham, for being utterly amazing.

Sophie Fisher, for telling me about Henry's mouse bait.

Charity Chen, for being my quick-as-lightning researcher.

CHAPTER ONE

Believing in Henry

you will know some things about me if you have read a book called *Alvin Ho: Allergic to Girls, School, and Other Scary Things*. But you won't know *all* about me, so that is why there is now this second book.

In case you missed it, my name is Alvin Ho. I was born scared and I am still scared. Things that scare me include:

Long words (especially "hippopotomonstrosesquipedaliophobia," which means fear of long words).

Punctuation. (Except for exclamation points! Exclamations are fantastic!!!)

The dark (which means I have nyctophobia).

The great outdoors. (What's so great about it?) Lots of things can happen when you're outdoors:

Hurricanes.

Tornadoes.

Mudslides.

Landslides.

The end of the world.

I am scared of many more things than that. But if I put all my scares on one list, it would mean years of therapy for me. And I already go to therapy once a month on account of it's supposed to help me not be so scared. But my brother Calvin says when you're born a certain way, that's the way you'll always be, so you might as well hug your inner scaredy-cat.

My brother Calvin, he gives good advice.

I am not so good with advice. I can never think of any, except maybe this: When in doubt, always ask, "What would Henry do?" Henry is Henry David Thoreau. He's a dead author, which is really creepy. But he is also our school hero, which is not so creepy, and he was a lot like me—he had stuff figured out, even when he was little. He was born in Concord, Massachusetts, just like me. And—gulp—he died in Concord too.

Of course, I could never say, "What would Henry do?" at school, where I never say anything. This is on account of school is mortifying. And when I am mortified, which means totally scared to death, I can't scream, I can't talk, I can't even grunt. Nothing comes out of my mouth, no matter how hard I try.

Having a lot in common with Henry can be very useful. For example, we learned in music class today that Henry played the flute. And whenever he played, a mouse would come to listen, and Henry would feed it with the extra pieces of cheese that he kept in his pocket.

"My brother has a flute," I told the gang on the bus after school. "He rented it for lessons . . . and we have cheese in the refrigerator."

"Let's go," said Pinky.

So when the bus stopped at the end of my driveway, the gang followed me to my house. Usually, it is a tricky business getting them to play with me unless it is Pinky's idea. Pinky is the biggest boy and the leader of the gang, and no one plays with me unless Pinky does.

Except for Flea. Flea plays with me no matter what. But the problem with Flea is that she's a girl. And girls are annoying.

Fortunately, my mom was at work and my gunggung, who comes to watch us after school, was fast asleep on the sofa. So I left the gang in the kitchen and tiptoed past the sofa . . . to fetch Calvin's flute from the top of the piano where he had put it for safekeeping. No problem.

The only problem was Anibelly. She's four, she's my sister, and she was wide awake, following me everywhere and getting in my way as usual.

"That's Calvin's," said Anibelly.

I stopped. I pretended I didn't see Anibelly. But it is hard not to see her. She's like a stoplight in the middle of my life and there's just no avoiding her. I can't go anywhere without going past her or taking her with me if I'm in a hurry.

"But Calvin's practicing his karate moves at Stevie's house," I said. "And I need his flute for a little experiment."

"What spearmint?" asked Anibelly.

"Well, you live in Concord, Massachusetts, don't you?" I asked.

Anibelly nodded.

"You believe in God and Henry David Thoreau, don't you?"

Anibelly nodded again.

"Well, then, if you keep quiet," I said, "I'll let you watch."

So Anibelly kept quiet.

First I put Calvin's flute together.

Then I went back into the kitchen where the gang was waiting and looked for some cheese.

Actually there was quite a lot of cheese, all chopped up and zipped inside a plastic bag. It was very yummy. And we were hungrier than a pack of starving mice. By the time we finished snacking, there were only a few crumbs left to put in my pocket. But I was sure that our teacher, Miss P, had said that Henry had *pieces* of cheese, not crumbs.

"I'd heard *pieces* too, not crumbs," said Sam, who usually always pays better attention in class than I do. "A mouse isn't going to come for crumbs."

So we cobbled all our crumbs together to make a *piece* of cheese, which I put in my pocket. Then I picked up Calvin's flute, put it to my lips and blew.

"Pshhhhhffffffffrrrrrrrrrr." It sounded like a sick worm blowing its nose. So I blew again, harder. *"Pshhhhhhrrrrrrrrrrrrrrr!"*

"Lemme try," said Pinky, snatching the flute and the piece of cobbled cheese from my pocket. *"Pssssssssuuurrrggggggh!"* He sounded worse than I did!

Then Nhia took a turn. Then Sam. Then Jules and Eli and Hobson. By the time Calvin's flute was finally passed to Flea, it was drooling worse than our dog, Lucy, on a hot day, and the cobbled cheese that ended up in her pocket was hardly recognizable as cheese, except for the smell.

Worse, there was no mouse anywhere. It was not a good sign.

Even worse, a car was pulling into our driveway with Calvin inside.

"You're busted now," said Anibelly.

"Alvin Ho!" said Flea. "This is gross! I'm going home."

Then Flea handed me the flute, picked up her backpack and marched off, just like that. If there is anything good about Flea it is this: She knows when to call it quits.

But the gang did not.

"The problem is that we need to be outside . . . in the *woods*," said Nhia, who can figure things out like a detective. "Henry took his flute on his walks in the *woods*, where there are not only mice, but chipmunks . . . and squirrels . . . and bats. That's how Henry did it."

"Who's coming to Walden Woods with me?" asked Pinky. No one moved. No one said a word. Then Pinky turned and headed for the door. "Last one there is a chicken butt!" he said. And before I knew it, the gang rushed out.

If I were not scared of the woods, or if I had had on my Firecracker Man gear, I would have run after them. Firecracker Man isn't afraid of anything, but I am afraid of everything, especially the woods—they are full of trees. And Walden Woods, behind my house, is the creepiest of all—it is full of big stones too, carved with the words of Henry David Thoreau and other—gulp—dead people. If you read their words and stay long enough, you can even feel them sitting around, having a chat.

Lucky for me, the gang forgot the flute.

But unlucky for me, Flea was right. Calvin's flute was really gross. It was sticky and slimy and dripping with drool. And I was holding it when Calvin came in, dressed to kill.

● ● ● ●

There are many advantages to being Calvin:

1. You're nine years old, almost ten.
2. You can haul firewood.

3. Your fingers fit in a bowling ball.

4. You can crash your bike without crying.

5. You can do karate.

6. You can kick my butt.

There is only one
advantage to being me:
1.

I'm not sure what it is yet, but there
must be something. . . .

Okay, I can clean a flute like nobody's
business.

And put it back in its case.

And put the case back where it belongs, for
safekeeping.

"Okay, Calvin?" I asked.

"Okay," said Calvin. But he was not okay. He
was still mad at me. So I gave him one of my best
carved sticks, which is supposed to be a walking
stick but is especially useful for digging holes in
the yard. Then Calvin, Anibelly and I ran outside.

Digging holes is fantastic! It makes you

forget your troubles. And when Calvin gets started, there's no telling what he will forget—usually, everything. He digs better than anybody. He's a regular backhoe.

So by the time the delivery truck screeched up our driveway and dropped off a big box—*thwuuuup!*—we were buds again. We dropped our sticks and ran over.

"To: Mr. Alvin Ho," said the label. Calvin karate-chopped the box and I tore it open with my bare hands. Inside—gasp—was "Houdini in a Box: Do-It-Yourself Escape Kit."

"Wow," said Calvin.

"What is it?" asked Anibelly.

"It's . . . ," said Calvin. "It's . . ."

Then Calvin said nothing.

I said nothing.

What do you say when the best thing that has ever happened to you just dropped in your driveway?

CHAPTER TWO

The Fantastic Straitjacket Escape

i ripped open the kit right there in the driveway. Inside, there were pencils, stickers, handcuffs, a handcuff key, a rope, a *Houdini's Greatest Escapes* DVD and a gold card.

Calvin whistled. "Dude!" he said.

"I bet it's from Uncle Dennis," said Anibelly.

And sure enough, there was another card that said

HAPPY
BIRTHDAY,
SPORT!
LOVE,
UNCLE DENNIS

It was not my birthday. But my uncle Dennis, who lives in Boston, didn't know that. He's a cool dude. He butters his toast on both sides. He can never remember our birthdays exactly, but he sends something whenever he *thinks* it's our birthday, which could happen more than once a year, and it is always a marvelous surprise.

I could hardly believe my eyes. Harry Houdini was the best escape artist in the history of the world, as everyone knows. His real name was Erik Weisz. And now, with a little practice . . . I could be the next Houdini!

Thoughts swirled in my head.

Leaves swirled in the yard.

"C'mon," said Calvin, "let's watch the DVD."

We rushed inside.

Houdini's Greatest Escapes was amazing. First Houdini was blindfolded. Then he was tied. Then he was handcuffed. Then he was roped, hanging upside down! But he wriggled and squiggled and

squirmed and—gasp—escaped! Then he was tied to a chair, handcuffed and roped . . . and he escaped again! It was spectacular!

"Let's try it!" said Calvin.

So we did. We tried it on Anibelly first; she is very useful in that way.

First we did the blindfold.

Then we did the handcuffs.

Then we used the rope.

Anibelly slipped out of everything faster than Harry Houdini! She was great!

Then Calvin tried it. He squirmed a little more than Anibelly, but he slipped out of everything quickly too.

Then it was my turn. And I slipped right out of the very big handcuffs too, on account of my hands are very small.

Calvin stopped. He rubbed his chin. "I don't think we're doing it right," he said. "Great escapes are supposed to be *hard*. Otherwise, they're not great escapes. They're just regular escapes."

"Oh."

"Something's missing from this kit," said Calvin, inspecting the box. "Houdini had something we don't. . . ."

"It's the arms," said Anibelly excitedly. "The shirt! The shirt with the funny arms!"

"That's it!" said Calvin. "The straitjacket!" He dumped the packing peanuts out of the box. But there was no straitjacket.

"No problem," said Calvin. "I'll make one."

Calvin is great. One of his talents is taking things apart to see how they work. His other talent is making things.

First he found an old shirt.

Then he found another old shirt.

He cut the sleeves from one and stitched them carefully to the sleeves of the other, until the shirt had extra-long sleeves.

It was fabulous!

First we tried it on Anibelly. We wrapped the long sleeves around her tummy and tied them in the back. Her arms are short—like two bicycle handles—on account of she's only four and nothing has really grown in yet except her teeth. So it didn't take long for her to wriggle free. It wasn't like she was a real escape artist or anything.

Then we tried it on Calvin. His arms are longer. In fact, he wriggled quite a bit. He rocked wildly, tied to a chair, just like Houdini, until he knocked himself over and nearly cracked his head. It was super-duper! Then Calvin popped out of the straitjacket too.

Finally it was my turn. "Wrap me up! Wrap me up!" I cried.

"Not so fast," said Calvin. "I need a little more practice."

"But it's my turn."

"But I'm going to be the Great Calvini!" said Calvin.

"No, you're not," I said.

"Yes, I am!" said Calvin.

"No, you're not!"

"Yes, I am."

"It's *my* kit," I said.

"But it's *my* straitjacket," said Calvin.

This was true. I didn't know how to sew. Calvin had learned to sew in Scouts, just in case one of them conked their head on a rock while camping and was bleeding to death and needed stitching.

Calvin was just about to conk me on the head, when . . .

"Caaaalvin!" my mom called. "Time for ka-raaaate, huuuurry, honey!"

Calvin is always practicing karate or going to lessons. He can punch a brick without crying. Someday he will walk on sizzling coals without screaming, he is very talented in that way. But I am not. Karate freaks me out. So I stay home with Anibelly. And YehYeh usually comes to take us to the library and then out for ice cream while Calvin is out hurting himself.

"YehYeh will be here in a minute," said my mom, poking her head into the living room. "Be sure to let him in."

"Okay," I said.

"Okay," said Anibelly.

Then Calvin was gone, just like that.

But his fantastic straitjacket was not. It was lying on the floor, doing nothing.

CHAPTER THREE

The Works

"**gimme the works,**" I told Anibelly. "I'm going to surprise YehYeh. He's going to be very impressed."

Anibelly put her right foot out, like in her favorite Hokey Pokey dance, and crossed her arms in front of her. "You mean *scared*?" she said.

"Yup," I said. I could hardly wait. When YehYeh is particularly impressed, he always says, "Alvin, there's a difference between impressing and scaring," which is the same as saying there's a difference between cleaning your room (impressive) and cleaning the whole house (scary). And when he is scared, YehYeh is just like me. His mouth opens, but nothing comes out.

"Make everything super-duper tight," I told Anibelly.

"Okay," said Anibelly.

Anibelly can tell directions with a compass, she can sing the Hokey Pokey and dance it at the same time, and mostly she says what's on her mind. She can also figure things out, I don't know how—like how to tie a triple knot that won't come loose.

Anibelly gave me the works. She wrapped my sleeves around me like a couple of boa constrictors around a sausage. Then she knotted the rope around everything. Then she made everything super-duper tight.

"Something's still missing . . . ," I said. But I couldn't put my toe on it.

"I know," said Anibelly. "Houdini was in a box, right?"

"That's it!" I said. So Anibelly guided me carefully down the stairs to the basement where there was a box that said "Dishwasher This Side UP," on one side, and on the other side, it said in Calvin's handwriting "Danger: Time Machine."

"Roll me in," I told Anibelly.

So she did. She rolled me in.

This box couldn't be nailed shut like Harry Houdini's, but it could be taped. "Lalalalalalalalala," sang Anibelly as she ran around the box with tape on a roller that just keeps spinning out, like super-duper strong spider's silk. Inside the box, it was warm and dark.

The tiny breathing holes that Calvin and Anibelly had punched with a pencil looked like stars in the night.

"Anibelly," I called out.

Anibelly stopped.

"It's very warm in here," I said. "And dark."

"I know," said Anibelly. "That's why my blankie's in there. It's the perfect place for a nap. Try it."

"But—"

"Don't worry," said Anibelly, "I've set the time machine so you can go back to see dinosaurs. You'll love it!"

"But—"

"Lalalalalalalala," sang Anibelly. "Lalalala-lalalala . . ."

The box felt like an oven. Worse, it was *smaller* than an oven. It was the size of a *dishwasher*.

I didn't feel so good. I could hardly breathe. I couldn't move. Worse, I had a couple of itches I couldn't reach.

Worst of all, I have claustrophobia. I forgot. Oops.

Normally, I do not go in the time machine at all. In fact, I have never been inside. Calvin and Anibelly made it, it's their thing, but it's not my thing. I'm allergic. Small, squishy spaces make it hard for me to breathe and *moong cha cha*, which means foggy in the head, in Chinese. Plus, it was pitch-black-dark-as-night, except for the tiny breathing holes, which really were no help at all.

"Anibelly!" I screamed. "Let me out!"

Dingdong! rang the doorbell.

Anibelly stopped.

She dropped her roll of tape.

"YehYeh?" she said. "YehYeh's here! Yippeee!"

Anibelly thumped up the stairs. "Lalalalalala-lalalala," she sang as she went.

"ANIBELLY!" I screamed at the top of my lungs. "COME BAAAAACK!"

"Hi, YehYeh!" I heard Anibelly say upstairs.

"Hello, Princess!" said YehYeh.

Then I heard the sound of a hug and a kiss, and Anibelly squealing as she got tossed in the air.

"Where's Alvin?" asked YehYeh.

"HERE!" I screamed. "LEMMMME OUT!!!"

"He's practicing his escapes," said Anibelly, "to surprise you."

"Is he?" YehYeh chuckled. "I knew that sooner or later he'd want to go to karate class with Calvin. Well, good for him!

"Are you ready for our afternoon together?"

"Yup!" said Anibelly.

"I WANT TO COME TOO!" I screamed. But there was only one problem. No sound had come out of my mouth since Anibelly went up the stairs. When I am totally freaked out, my voice is all in my head, and my tongue feels like a million pieces of broken glass.

There was the rustle of Anibelly's coat going on.

Then the *clack, clack* of Anibelly's shoes.

"WAAAAAAIT!" I cried. "WAIT FOR MEEEEEE!"

"It sure is quiet without the boys around," chuckled YehYeh.

"Sure is," said Anibelly.

Then the door slammed.

"Come BAAAAAAAAAAAAAAAACK!" I cried.

Silence.

In fact, the silence was so enormous you'd think I was swallowed by a dishwasher box or something.

CHAPTER FOUR

Inspector of Snowstorms and Rainstorms

crying is really great. It makes you very tired. And when you run out of tears, you can just go to sleep.

So I did.

I went to sleep in the time machine headed for the Mesozoic Era where I was going to be scared to death, but at least I was going to see the deinonychus leap on its prey and wrap its long arms and three-fingered hands around it and kick it to death with its sickle-shaped toenails.

But when I rolled out of the time machine, there were no dinosaurs anywhere, only a boy, about Calvin's size, looking at me, blinking. He had a backpack over his shoulder and a smooth stick in his hand.

"Are you a crazy person or a prisoner?" he asked.

I said nothing. I don't talk to strangers.

"Well, either way, I thought you were dead," he said. "I was hoping to collect you as a specimen."

I wasn't dead. But I was lying in Calvin's straitjacket in the leaves in the woods.

"I am Inspector of Snowstorms and Rainstorms," said the boy.

I stopped. I sat up. It sounded familiar. It was a nickname for someone I knew, but I couldn't remember who. I looked at him sideways.

"Are you an Indian?" asked the boy.

I shook my head.

"Are you a Chinaman?"

I shook my head again.

"Can you speak?"

I nodded.

"Do you like birds?"

I nodded. "I like dinosaurs better."

"I like dinosaurs too," he said. "But I'm afraid I haven't got any dinosaur eggs today."

He rummaged in his backpack and pulled out a box made from strips of bark. Inside were little eggs.

"Let's hatch these," he said. "You know how to hatch eggs, don't you?"

I shook my head no.

"You sit on them, of course," said Inspector. He quickly collected twigs and bark and moss and made a couple of nests. Then he divided the eggs, and we sat on top of them.

"I just love it here in the woods," he said. "My dad takes me hiking and camping all the time. Don't you just love it too?"

I shook my head no. The woods are creepy. Really creepy.

I looked around. There were trees everywhere.

"Time to rotate your eggs," said Inspector. "A mother bird will rotate her eggs many times a day."

I rotated my eggs. Then I sat back down.

"A Nashville warbler's egg takes eleven to twelve days to hatch," said Inspector, reading from a large book. "A short-eared owl's, about a month."

It was not good news.

But then I felt something. "My eggs are ready," I blurted.

Inspector stopped. He looked up.

"They're about to hatch!" I cried. My heart was thumping faster than a hummingbird's.

"How do you know?"

"Because it feels different," I said.

"Different?"

I got up. There was yolk and egg all over my butt. "C'mon," said Inspector, "my mom will take care of you."

We hurried out of the woods . . . and down the street . . . but it wasn't a street exactly, it was a dirt path. There weren't any of the usual houses along the street . . . it was very strange.

There were no cars.

No streets.

No noise.

Nothing.

"HEY, WAS THERE AN ALIEN AB-DUCTION OR SOMETHING?" I yelled. "WHERE ARE ALL THE CARS? WHERE DID THE STREETS GO?"

Things didn't get any better when we got to Inspector's house.

"David Henry Thoreau!" said his mother. "Skipping school again? And getting a friend in trouble too!" She looked at me.

"You're lucky it's wash day," she said to me. Then she began to tear my clothes off.

Off went Calvin's strait-jacket.

Off went my pants.

David Henry Thoreau? She didn't mean *Henry David Thoreau*, did she? I turned and looked at Inspector.

My heart stopped.

My mouth opened.

He looked just like the Henry poster on our classroom wall!

I wanted to scream, but nothing came out.

I would have liked traveling back 200 million years to see the deinonychus tearing its prey, but going back almost two hundred years to meet a dead author was enough to scare me right into my grave.

I needed to get home—fast! So I turned and shot out the door and ran as fast as I could go, up the dirt road and into the woods, my butt as naked as cake without frosting.

CHAPTER FIVE

Acts of God

"**aaaaaaaaaaaaaaaack!**" I jolted awake.

Someone was rattling my box. "Anibelly?"

"Noooooooooo!" I cried.

"Alvin???" came my dad's voice through the holes. "What are you doing in Anibelly's nap place?"

"*Waaaaaaaaaaaaaaaaaaaaaaaaaaah!*" I wailed. "*Waaaaaaaaaah!*" Crying is great. You always feel better afterward, especially when you've traveled four hundred years round-trip in a small, en-closed time machine.

"What happened to you?" my dad asked, rip-ping open the box with his bare hands.

My dad is *da dad.* He's saved my life at least seven hundred and fourteen times eight, and mostly in the nick of time, right as I come upon the pearly gates and take a number to stand in line and wait my turn.

"I . . . I . . . I . . ." I didn't know where to begin. So I didn't. Instead, I fell like candy from a wrap-per into my dad's arms and sobbed. And he hugged me back like I was the best thing he'd ever found in a box.

My dad isn't a superhero, but he can pull me out of anything, even from long, tangled boa constrictors that were squeezing the last wheeze out of me.

"You get yourself into such binds," he said, peeling the straitjacket off of me.

"You're my best friend, Dad. You saved my life."

Then I told him all about traveling in the time machine and meeting Henry David Thoreau.

"It was really creepy," I said, sniffling. "But Henry was okay. He really loved nature, Dad.

"He collected specimens . . .

"He had eggs that we tried hatching . . .

"And a big book on birds . . .

"And a walking stick . . .

"He said his dad took him camping and hiking *all* the time."

Of course, I left out the part about getting egg on my butt on account of it was way too embarrassing.

My dad didn't say anything. He just listened. My mom says she married him because he's such a great listener. You can drop all your words into his ears for safekeeping and none of them will ever get lost. I think it has something to do with being a gentleman—my dad knows all the rules—but I'm not really sure, I don't remember.

"Son," my dad finally said. I love it when he calls me that. Son. I love it more than my own name.

My dad's eyes were as shiny as pennies in vinegar. "Henry's father gave him a wonderful gift," he continued, "a gift every father should give his children."

"What gift?" I asked. I like gifts.

"A love of nature," said my dad.

"That's a gift?"

"One of the finest," said my dad. "To know and appreciate nature is the key to a lifetime of discovery."

My dad looked at me.

I looked at my dad.

"I know nature," I said. It was true. I watch it all the time on TV. There's nothing I don't know about nature:

Earthquakes.

Landslides.

Mudslides.

Floods.

Hurricanes.

Tsunamis.

Tornadoes.

Volcanic eruptions.

Meteorites.

When it comes to nature, I'm practically an entire Web site!

"Why don't you and I go camping this weekend, son?"

"Camping?"

"It would be good for you to be in the great outdoors," said my dad. "You will learn some skills. It will give you confidence. You'll see that the woods is not such a scary place."

Gulp.

"Fall is the best time to camp," my dad continued. "Spring's too wet. Summer's too hot. Winter's too cold. But in the fall, the leaves are showing off their colors, the days are still warm, the air is crisp. It was my favorite time to camp when I was about your age. . . ."

"They used to call me One-Match Jack," my dad added, puffing out his chest. "Do you know why?"

I shook my head. His name wasn't Jack.

"Because I could start a fire with one match," he said. "One match. Imagine that."

My dad looked at me. "You can do that too," he said. "We'll make our own shelter . . . catch our own fish . . . I'll even show you how to make a pit toilet."

"A pit what?"

"It may be the beginning of a lifelong hobby," said my dad. "You could come back a changed man."

"But I'm not a man," I squeaked. "And we might not come back at all!

"We could get lost in the leaves!

"There could be a freak blizzard, and we could get lost in the snow!

"Or a flash flood, and we could be drowned!

"Or we could get struck by lightning!

"We could die by meteorite!"

Silence.

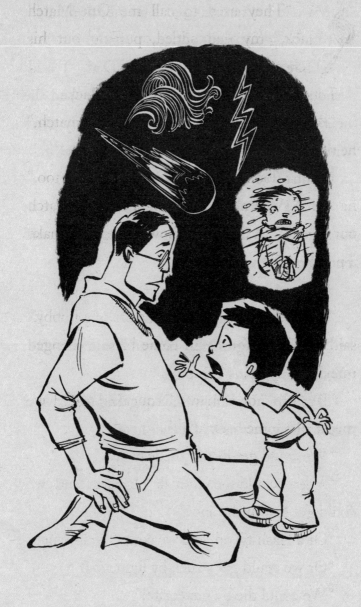

My dad looked stunned. His mouth opened. But nothing came out.

"They're called acts of God, Dad," I said. "And when they happen, they happen. And the next thing you know, you're at the pearly gates with a number in your hand, waiting to get in."

"Don't worry—" my dad began.

"Don't worry?" I said. "Millions die at once in an act of God! It's the worst way to go. We could be in line forever!"

"In line?" asked my dad.

"To get into heaven!" I said.

"You're not going to heaven," said my dad. "You're only going camping."

"I'm not?" I swallowed. Not going to heaven? It was the worst news I'd ever heard.

CHAPTER SIX

Grow a Beard and Live Like an Animal

"**whatcha doin'?**" asked Flea on the school bus the next day. She is my desk buddy at school, and sometimes she is also my bus buddy. I think she likes sitting next to me, that is when she's not mad at me.

"Nuttin'," I muttered. I covered my paper with my arm.

The windows on the bus went *clackity-clack.*

"C'mon," said Flea. "Lemme see."

"No," I said.

"C'mon," said Flea. "I'll give you a Haw

Flake." She had a piece of candy in the shape of a quarter between her finger and thumb.

Haw Flakes are my favorite. They grow on hawthorn trees in China. Flea had her first Haw Flake at my house, and now she has Haw Flakes all the time. Where she gets them, I have no idea.

I snatched the sweet and popped it quick into my mouth. Then I showed her my list:

How to avoid a Bear Attack
1. Don't go camping.
2. Don't go anywhere near a camp.
3. Don't even THINK of camping.

"Are you going camping?" asked Flea.

"Not if I can help it," I said. "But my dad says he's taking me this weekend."

"Camping's terrific!" said Flea.

"You mean terrifying," I said.

"You'll have a great time," said Flea, "if it's anything like the camp I went to."

"You've camped?" I asked.

"Sure have," said Flea. "It was at a camp for kids like me."

I looked at Flea sideways.

"You, know, kids with irregular arms or legs or prosthetics!" said Flea.

Flea is so lucky. She is blind in one eye, which makes her look like a pirate, and extra-long in one leg, which she drags like a genuine peg leg.

"We played games, went swimming and horseback riding, did archery and made crafts," Flea added. "At night, when it was dark, we sang songs around the campfire and roasted marshmallows."

"That isn't camp," said Eli, turning around in his seat. "That's a country club."

"Yeah, girls don't know anything about camping," said Nhia. "If Alvin's dad is taking him, it means he's going *real* camping."

"Real camping," said Pinky, who is the biggest boy because he started kindergarten late, and is an expert on everything, "is roughing it."

"No electricity," said Jules. "Just flashlights."

"No TV, no video games, no e-mail," said Sam.

"You grow a beard and live like an animal," said Eli.

"You either get hit by lightning, or you don't," whispered Hobson.

"If you can't start a fire, you could freeze to death," added Scooter. "If you do start a fire, you could burn to death."

"If you hear a rattler, it's too late," said Pinky. "*Sssssssssssssss.*"

"And when it's over," added Sam, "the Angel of Death comes for you!"

The boys on the bus breathed in and out.

The driver's eyes in the mirror looked up and down.

"Alvin can't do that kind of camping, can you, Alvin?" Pinky sneered.

Heads turned.

All eyes were on me.

The seats on the bus went *bumpity-bump*.

"Stand up for yourself, Alvin," said Flea. "He's just jealous."

I would have stood up for myself, but I didn't feel so good.

I was hardly breathing.

Kindergarten and first grade flashed before my eyes.

Camping sounded worse than I had imagined.

Way worse.

CHAPTER SEVEN

Sitting in Your Underwear Is a Little Boring

the problem with having camping on your mind is that you can't think about anything else. Everything is sort of a blur.

"Commas are very useful," I heard Miss P say. She is our teacher. She is very smart. She knows a lot about everything.

"When writing a letter, use a comma after the person's name in the greeting," Miss P continued. It was writing class.

"And before you sign your name at the bottom of the letter, use a comma after the closing," said Miss P. "Remember to say good-bye in a friendly way." She wrote examples on the board:

Your friend,

Yours truly,

Love,

See you soon,

Sincerely,

No problem. Commas are cute. They look like a smile standing up. Or they could be a mustache. Or the handle on an apple. Or a fingernail clipping. Or an eyebrow. Or the side of a zipper, if you make a bunch of them together like this,,,,,,,,,,,,,,,,,,,,,,,. You can even make a rather long zipper,,, ,,.

"Now we will practice writing a letter to the person next to you," said Miss P, interrupting my concentration. "Remember to use commas."

Flea bent over our desk so that I couldn't see what she was writing. She wrote so furiously, she sounded like a pencil factory.

In fact, the entire class sounded like a pencil factory. I sank into my chair. I squeezed my eyes

shut and wished with
all my might that I
was my superhero
self, Firecracker
Man! He would
blast out of writing
class in a shower of
sparks and gunpowder!

But I couldn't.

And Flea just kept on writing.

So there was nothing else for me to do but load up my commas and fire away:

Dear Flea, your breath smells like black
   lickrish,,,,,,,,,,
To my nose it is very ticklish,,,,,,,,,,
So don't eat lickrish when you're camping,,,,,,,,,,,
Or the bear will end up
   cramping,,,,,,,,,,,,,,,,,,
With you inside feeling quite picklish!!!!!!!!!

"Miss Peeeeeee!" cried Flea. "Alvin's doing it all wrong."

Miss P came over. She stopped. She bent over my desk. "Alvin," she said.

I really had it coming.

"Why, Alvin!" cried Miss P. "You've written a limerick!" She sounded very pleased.

So I sat up.

"What's a limerick?" asked Flea.

"A limerick is a funny poem," said Miss P. "It rhymes and tells a story."

I swung my feet. I kept my eyes low. I kept my hands in plain sight. I thought I had written a letter. It was the kind of letter my dad would write to my mom, except without all the commas. She had a whole collection of them on the refrigerator door.

"We could have an entire lesson on limericks!" said Miss P. Her eyes were sparkling like marbles in the sun. It was not a good sign.

Fortunately, the recess bell rang and we all jumped out of our seats.

It was a very close call.

The best thing about recess is that it doesn't matter if you are having trouble paying attention in class. Suddenly, you are paying attention to a million things on the playground.

"Let's play camping," Pinky announced as soon as we got outside. Since he's the leader of the gang, he gets to say what the gang plays.

"The first thing we have to do is pitch a tent by a bubbling brook," said Pinky. "Then we'll catch a few frogs. Then we'll make a roaring fire. After that, we'll paddle a canoe and go fishing."

Camping isn't like the games where you choose sides and someone gets left out. Everyone plays together. So we pitched an imaginary tent on the kickball field. Then we paddled our imaginary canoe and fished. Then some of us turned into bears and chased the

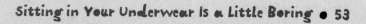

campers. Then the campers roared and chased the bears. It was terrific!

Camping was not scary at all, until . . . the girls wanted to play.

"Go away," said Pinky. "No girls allowed."

"That's discrimination," said Esha.

"It's not," said Sam. "We're just camping."

"That's not camp-
ing," said Sara Jane.

"No one camps on
asphalt," said Ophelia.

Then the girls began
to giggle.

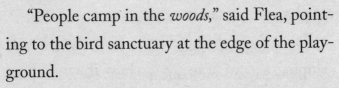

"People camp in the *woods*," said Flea, point-ing to the bird sanctuary at the edge of the play-ground.

The gang turned and stared. Usually, no one goes there except to do a class project with the art teacher or science teacher. It is a little scary.

"We knew that," said Pinky. "We were just warming up. Right, guys?"

Silence.

Then before I knew it, everyone was running

toward the bird sanctuary. When we got there, the girls ran right in. But the boys stopped.

It wasn't as bad as it looked from a distance. There were trees, a little breeze and birds chirping. But it was kind of *dark* in there.

"What are the boys waiting for?" a girl's voice drifted out.

"Maybe they're scared," said another.

Then they giggled.

That was it. The boys hurled themselves into the bird sanctuary, except for me. I'm allergic. So I stayed at the edge of the playground where I could watch everything *and* keep an eye out for the playground monitor, just in case.

Fortunately, the boys knew everything about camping and were ready to show the girls how it's done.

Pitching a tent was no problem. Nhia suggested taking off their shirts and pants and tying them together to make a tent. It was brilliant! Who would have ever thunk it? It was a much better tent than the girls', which was only a bunch of sticks leaning against a tree like a teepee.

"It's called a lean-to," said Flea. "I learned it at camp."

"You mean a bean-to?" asked Pinky. "Looks like you're all waiting for beans to grow up the poles!"

Pinky was right. A bunch of sticks isn't a tent at all!

"Betcha can't make a fire," said Jules, who was playing on the girls' side.

"Betcha can't either," said Hobson.

Then everyone rushed around gathering sticks and leaves and pieces of wood for a fire. It was the boys against the girls.

But starting a fire was harder than rubbing two sticks together.

It was even harder than using a magnifying glass, which no one had, so the boys used Eli's glasses, which were good for nothing, not even for inspecting ants.

Nothing worked. (It was a good thing the girls' fire didn't work either.)

And sitting around in your underwear in

front of an imaginary fire is a little boring. So Pinky said why didn't they climb trees? "Girls can't climb as good as boys," he yelled.

And Pinky was right! All the boys went up, up, up, much faster and higher than the girls.

"C'mon, Alvin," shouted Sam. "Climb with us!"

I didn't move. I have acrophobia. I couldn't join them, but watching the boys climb was almost as exciting as putting snakes in a bag!

Watching the girls, however, was boring. They didn't climb very far.

"You win!" said Flea.

"Yeah," said Esha. "I don't like heights."

"Neither do I," said Orphelia.

"It's for the birds," said Flea.

"And the boys," added Sara Jane.

Then they giggled.

Worse, the bell rang. Recess was over.

And because they were the losers and not very far from the ground, the girls jumped down and ran.

But the boys did not.

"Camping is g-g-great," said Pinky.

"You're l-l-lucky to be going c-c-camping with your d-d-dad," stammered Sam.

"You'll have a great t-t-time," said Scooter.

I nodded. I sure was lucky. I was on the ground.

They were high in the trees.

And they were stuck.

"I need the b-b-bathroom," said Pinky.

"Me too," said Scooter.

"Help!" yelled Eli.

"HEEEEEEEEELLLLP!" screamed Nhia. "Somebody HEEEEEEELLLLP!"

"Lemmeeee DOWWWWWWN!" shrieked Hobson.

I wished that I could help them, but I couldn't. So I turned and ran. I had to tell someone, fast!

But when I got back inside, my mouth felt like it was full of sand. I couldn't say anything at all. And Miss P told me to take a seat. It was time for class to begin.

"Where are the boys?" asked Miss P. She looked around. It was strangely quiet without them.

"Camping," said Flea.

"Camping?" Miss P looked puzzled. Then she looked at me. I was the only boy in the class, except for maybe Jules, but no one can tell whether Jules is a boy or a girl. "Jules" could stand for "Julian" or it could stand for "Julia."

I kept my hands in plain sight.

I said nothing.

But my eyes can talk when my mouth can't. My eyes looked out the window, far away across the playground and into the bird sanctuary, where you could almost see underwear clinging to the tops of the trees if you looked really hard.

Miss P figured it out. Like I said, she's very smart. And when the fire truck from the Concord Fire Engine Co. came screaming into the playground, everyone poured out of the school to watch.

If I could have given the gang some advice, it would have been this: It's important to have already used the bathroom before climbing trees.

CHAPTER EIGHT

A Few Things to Pack

time was running out.

"Here's a few things to pack for our trip," my dad said after dinner. He handed me a list:

1. Flashlight
2. Batteries
3. Whistle
4. Mirror
5. Sunscreen
6. Insect repellent
7. Anti-itch lotion
8. First-aid kit
9. Compass

I read the list. I was not impressed.

"If you think of other things, go ahead and pack them," said my dad. "But keep it simple. It's only for two days."

Two *whole* days?

"I can't wait," said my dad, giving my shoulder a squeeze. "A little hiking, a little camping—maybe even a little fishing—we're going to love being in the great outdoors together."

"I love being together with you anyway, Dad," I said. I squeezed his shoulder back. I think it's a gentleman thing to do, like shaking hands, only fewer germs.

"I love being with you too, Alvin," said my dad. "It'll be a great *adventure*."

"What if we get lost?" I asked.

"Then we'll use our compasses."

"What if our compasses are lost?"

"Then I'll show you how to make one with a watch and a match."

"What if it rains ALL day and night and all the next day and night too?"

"Then we will huddle together and drink hot chocolate."

"What if something happens to you, Dad?"

"Then you will rescue me, son."

Silence.

"I will?"

"I know you will."

"What if I get sick?" I asked.

"Then we'll come home," said my dad.

"No . . . I mean, what if I get sick *before* we leave?"

My dad blinked. He looked at me.

"Major suffering," I said. "A leave-me-for-dead whopper."

"What did you have in mind?" my dad asked.

"Measles–mumps–rubella–typhoid–malaria–scarlet fever–Black Death–campophobia."

"Sorry I asked," said my dad.

"Then we'd have to cancel, right, Dad?"

"*Ohhhhhhhh,*" my dad groaned. He put his head in his hands.

I didn't know what to say.

I scratched my butt.

I looked at my list.

Then I ran to find Calvin.

••••

Calvin is amazing.

He knows something about everything.

"A ferrule is the metal band on a pencil that holds the eraser in place," Calvin said, reading from the computer screen in our room, with Anibelly next to him. They were both in their pajamas. So I got into mine.

"The father of Harry Houdini was a rabbi." Calvin's eyes moved across the bright screen.

"What's a rabbi?" I asked.

"It's a rabbit without the 't,'" said Calvin. "I think they meant he was a rabbit." He was reading the entire encyclopedia online and he was up to the letter "F." But he also liked to skip around.

"Did you know that bats always turn left when leaving a cave?"

"Even Batman?" I asked.

"Dunno about that one," said Calvin. "The bite of the taipan snake can kill you within three seconds, but the bite of the tiger snake can take up to twelve hours.

"Do you want to know about spider bites?"

"Yes," said Anibelly.

"No," I said.

"Why not?" asked Calvin.

"Because I have arachnophobia," I said. "And I'm going camping."

Fortunately, it was time for Anibelly to go to

bed. So I waited until she left the room, and then I showed Calvin my list.

He helped me make some improvements:

World's best
1. Flashlight
2. ~~Batteries~~ Generator
3. ~~Whistle~~ Siren
4. ~~Mirror~~ Search beam
5. ~~Sunscreen~~ SPF 70
6. ~~Insect repellent~~ Jungle-grade netting
7. ~~A~~ ~~situation~~ Toilet paper
8. ~~First aid kit~~ Trauma dressing kit
9. ~~Compass~~ GPS

It was great!

Calvin added a few extras for just in case. Then he helped me find everything online.

We went to www.campwithoutfear.com, and with just a few clicks, we were set.

"Will everything get here in time?" I asked.

"No problem," said Calvin. "Next Day Delivery."

"Will it cost a lot of money?" I asked.

"None," said Calvin. "I'll use Dad's credit card. He said it's for emergency use only—and this is an emergency."

I nodded.

"This way no one has to spend any money," Calvin explained, "you pay with plastic."

My brother Calvin is really, truly amazing. He knows everything.

"Thanks, Calvin," I said.

"No problem," said Calvin.

Then we went to bed and turned out the light.

It was very, very dark.

Maybe it was as dark as camping in the woods.

And it was very quiet.

"I'm still afraid of going camping, Calvin," I whispered.

Silence.

"Cal?"

"It's okay to be scared," said Calvin, his voice

fading into dreams. "What matters is that you have the right stuff."

Zzzzzzzzzzzzzzzzzzzzzzzzzz.

"Okay," I said. But I was not okay. I was wide awake. And I was worried about a million things.

What if the wrong package arrives and I get a bunch of lightbulbs or plastic flowers or candle holders?

What if the right package arrives but none of the stuff works?

What if the stuff works but I forget to take it with me?

What if I remember to take the stuff but don't know how to use it?

The hairs on my head stuck out like a raccoon cap struck by lightning. Then I remembered— my uncle Dennis was coming to watch us after school the next day, and if anyone knows anything about the right stuff and how to use it, it's my uncle Dennis.

After that I felt much better. Then I finally closed my eyes, and the hairs on my head went to sleep too.

CHAPTER NINE

Dryer Lint Can Save Your Life

my uncle dennis arrived before Next Day Delivery. He is very quick that way; it is one of his talents. He is also highly trained in unarmed combat, snowball combat, wrapping-paper-roll combat, combat without combat, signals, rolling stops and emergency landings.

Uncle Dennis can tell some great stories, but he can never finish them. He always stops halfway on account of "the rest of it is *so bad*, I'd give away some illegal doings," he says. He's a secret agent of some sort, I'm sure of it. Just look at his Batman ring. It's a dead giveaway!

And he can sense when a suspicious package is about to arrive. "The delivery truck is coming up your driveway," said Uncle Dennis. "Is it your birthday?"

"I hope so," I said.

Thwuuuuuump!

It was my Next Day Delivery!

Anibelly and I pushed the box into the kitchen and ripped it open.

This is what we found:

The Monster Eye. Not just any monster eye, but the super-duper Triple Action Monster Eye Wide Beam Flashlight, to be exact.

A portable diesel generator for disaster use.

A GPS.

And a bunch of extra stuff that Calvin had added at the last minute:

N95 respirator dust masks.

Water-purification tablets.

Energy bars.

Night-vision goggles.

"Whoa!" said Uncle Dennis, trying on the night-vision goggles. "Son of a water pistol!" He was very impressed. And it takes a lot to impress my uncle Dennis.

He looked at all the stuff. Then he looked at me. Then he lowered his voice.

"You're a little worried about camping with your dad, aren't you?" he asked.

"Not a little worried," I cried, "I'm all freaked out!"

Uncle Dennis took a deep breath. He cracked his knuckles.

"Camping's not that bad," he said. "All you need are some secret tips. Just remember what SURVIVAL spells:

" 'S'—size up the situation.

" 'U'—use all your senses.

" 'R'—relieve yourself first.

" 'V'—veer from fear and panic.

" 'I'—improvise.

" 'V'—vacuum your crumbs.

" 'A'—always carry some form of weapon on you.

" 'L'—Learn some secret tricks.

" 'L' is the most important one," said Uncle Dennis, who is an expert on secret tricks. He can take nearly anything and make it useful in many different ways. It is something he learned in secret agent training school, I'm sure of it.

"Secret Trick Number One," said my uncle Dennis. "Dryer lint can save your life."

"Dryer lint?" My mouth fell open and Anibelly's Hokey Pokey toe went out.

"It catches fire with a single spark," said Uncle Dennis. "It's also light and easy to pack."

So then Anibelly and I collected dryer lint. It was easy!

"Secret Trick Number Two," said my uncle Dennis, leading us into the backyard. "Trapping dinner is easier than hunting it."

Uncle Dennis tied a rope around our littlest tree and pulled it until the entire tree bent over in a question mark. With the other end of the rope, he made a big loop, like a noose, and pinned it to the ground with a heavy rock. "Young trees are very flexible," he explained. "When you bend it over you can set the other end of the rope into a trap, like this."

Anibelly watched Uncle Dennis very carefully.

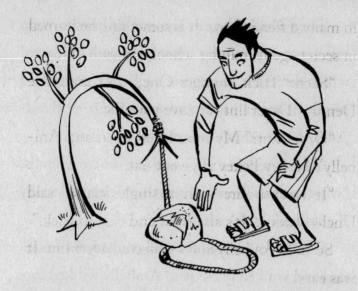

"This is called the dangle trap," said Uncle Dennis. "When your prey steps into the rope and loosens it from the rock, the tree will snap itself upright and dangle the prey."

"Does it hurt?" asked Anibelly, frowning.

"Probably not," said Uncle Dennis. "This is different from traps that mangle, tangle and strangle. But it will surprise."

"Hooray!" said Anibelly. "I like surprises."

"Then you'll like Secret Trick Number Three," said Uncle Dennis. "Toilet paper has many uses. You can use it to wrap, tape and signal."

Then Uncle Dennis showed us how to wrap toilet paper around a tree or branch to signal which direction we're going. Then we dampened pieces of toilet paper and used them as Band-Aids on our scratches and mosquito bites.

"Most importantly," said my uncle Dennis, "wipe with it. Don't use anything else, especially if you don't know what it is."

Uncle Dennis nodded and winked. So I nodded and winked back. And Anibelly winked too. She doesn't miss a thing.

"Secret Trick Number Four: Mosquito netting makes a good hammock." He strung the jungle-grade mosquito netting between two trees.

"Secret Trick Number Five: Marshmallows can give you a peaceful night's sleep." Uncle Dennis dashed into the kitchen and came back with a bag of marshmallows. He stuffed a marshmallow into each ear. Earplugs! What a fantastic idea!

Anibelly and I ate some marshmallows and stuffed our ears with them, and Lucy's too. Then we ran around the yard screaming at the top of our lungs. We could hardly hear, but we chased one another until our toilet paper Band-Aids fell off and a couple of our marshmallows popped out. After that, we took some sticks and dug some holes in the yard. Digging holes is great!

When we finally made it back to Uncle Dennis, he was motionless in the hammock, marshmallows in his ears, fast asleep.

"What's Secret Trick Number Six?" I asked.

Uncle Dennis did not stir. But he moaned, just a little.

I held my breath.

My uncle Dennis is a sleep talker and will spill all sorts of secrets when he's in stage two light sleep. Sleep talking is sure to give you away if you're a secret agent. That is why when secret agents get captured, they have to stay awake no matter what.

"Listen, Sport . . . ," mumbled Uncle Dennis.
I gasped.

"You don't . . . need so many . . . secret tips. . . .
All you . . . need is a . . . special secret . . .
weapon."

A special secret weapon? Now the truth was
out. I shivered in my sneakers.

Uncle Dennis's hand reached for the chain
around his neck.

I gasped again.

"Forget . . . the . . . equipment," his words

floated out between dreams. "*This* is . . . all you . . . need." His BATMAN RING dropped from his chain into my hand!

I was speechless. I slipped the black rubbery Batman ring on my finger. It fit perfectly!

"You gotta . . . be like . . . Batman," spilled Uncle Dennis. "You gotta . . . believe . . . in your own . . . secret Batpowers."

I nodded. It was all I could do. My uncle Dennis is really amazing. This proved, once and for all, that he was the real thing. A genuine, indestructible, top-secret secret agent.

And now I had his secret weapon.

CHAPTER TEN

The Secret Powers of My Batman Ring

this is what happens when you wear a Batman ring:

You can fly like a bat, turning left out of the Batschool, and be the first on the playground for recess.

You can hang upside down on the monkey bars forever.

You can see in the dark.

You can emit sonar waves.

But you still can't pay attention in class. In fact, it's even harder than ever to concentrate. You just keep thinking about all the fantastic things you can do now that you're wearing a Batman ring.

It was reading class. Reading class is better than writing class, but it still takes a lot of concentration. Everyone takes turns reading, which means you have to move your finger right along the words and not lose your place. This is hard to do.

It is even harder to do when you're a bat and your fingers are all webbed together.

The other problem with reading when you're a bat is your eyes. Bat eyes are very good for reading in the dark, but they are horrible at reading in the light. No matter how hard you squint, your beady eyes might as well be a couple of useless marbles in your head. The only thing that still works for a bat in reading class is his ears.

"Alvin?"

I twisted my Batman ring.

It was Miss P. She is very nice, but she has a

habit of calling on you when you least expect it. "It's your turn, honey."

Honey? My bat fur melted a little. My toes loosened from the bar under my chair. I swung in the breeze.

I can't read out loud in class. My voice doesn't work. But Miss P calls on me anyway, just to be fair. She is very nice. Especially when she calls me honey.

The hand on the clock clicked *tick, tick, tick.*

Somewhere a bat wing went *tap, tap, tap.*

Miss P waited patiently. Then she moved on.

"Fauntleroy?" Miss P called on Pinky. That is his real name. It's not the best name in the world, but it's all he's got, besides Pinky.

Pinky is not a great reader, but normally he reads okay.

But today, Pinky was not normal.

He shifted his beady eyes. He showed his vampire teeth.

Silence.

"Sam?" called Miss P.

Silence.

"Eli?

"What's going on with the boys today?" asked Miss P. "All the girls have read wonderfully, but you boys are acting very strange."

"They're bats," said Flea, who was sitting next to me. She sees more things out of her one good eye than most people see out of two.

"Bats?" said Miss Flea. "You mean they're *pretending* to be bats?"

"No, Miss P," said Flea. "I mean they're *real* bats."

"Oh."

"And bats can't read in the light," Flea added, matter-of-factly. "Their eyes don't work that way. They can only read in the dark."

"It all started with Alvin's ring," said Sara Jane. "Then all the boys made rings like it in art class."

"Oh?" Miss P looked over at the clay rings pinched on the boys' fingers. Then she strolled over to my desk.

I kept my eyes low. I kept my hands in plain sight. When you are wearing bling, it is important to act as normal as possible.

Miss P's eyes fell on my hand. She gasped. "A Batman ring! I haven't seen one since I was about your age.

"Mine had a special secret power that melted evil villains on the spot," she added.

"My ring can melt UFOs," said Scooter.

"And my ring can melt monsters," said Nhia.

"My ring can melt the principal!" blurted Hobson.

Oops.

"Why don't we put the rings away for safe-keeping?" said Miss P. "You can have them back

at the end of the day." Before we knew it, all our bat rings were in her desk, including my one-and-only true, genuine, authentic, real Batman ring that started it all.

I twisted a phantom ring on my finger. It felt terrible.

My mom says that it is Miss P's first year of teaching and that I should always be on my best behavior on account of Miss P might not know what to do if I am not, but she knew what to do with my Batman ring, that's for sure.

School was no fun after that.

"It's a good idea to keep our valuables at home," said Miss P when I finally went to her desk to pick up my Batman ring at the end of the day. "You wouldn't want to lose something like that. You'll need it to protect yourself from much scarier things than school."

Much scarier things than school?

What could be much scarier than school?

I scratched my side.

Then I scratched the back of my neck.

Then I remembered.

CHAPTER ELEVEN

I, Alvin, Being of Scaredy Mind...

this is how to know you're going to die. It is a sure sign.

Your mom cooks your favorite meal.

"Vegetable wonton and noodles, just for you," said my mom, who is really super-duper. She can smile and talk and cook at the same time and not spill anything, just like the people on cooking shows.

Normally, I would run around the house like crazy in my Firecracker Man outfit and scream

at the top of my lungs for vegetable wonton and noodles. The whole house gets steamy and smells like a wonton factory and there is a big, marvelous mess all over the kitchen.

But this was not normal. We were leaving for our camping trip in the morning. This was my Last Supper! It happened to Jesus and the gang in the Bible and now it was happening to me.

And after one eats one's Last Supper, there really isn't much left to do but—gulp—die. But since I had some time before that happened, Calvin said that I could write my Last Will and

Testament, to make sure that my belongings go to the right people after I am gone.

So right before bed, and with a little help from Calvin, I wrote in my best handwriting:

My Last Will and Testament

I, Alvin, being of scaredy mind and scaredier body, hereby leave to my brother, Calvin, the following:

My old toothbrush (I'm taking my new one with me)

~~my silver dollar~~

~~my Houdini kit.~~

all my socks under my bed.

And to my sister, Anibelly, I leave:

my carved sticks collection

one piece of sea glass

~~my Firecracker Man outfit, maybe~~

To my dog, Lucy, I leave my tennis balls

To my dad I leave my baseball glove, maybe.

And to my mom,

I hadn't finished yet when Calvin interrupted.

"That's not a very good Last Will and Testament," said Calvin. He was reading over my shoulder.

"Why not?"

"Because I'd rather have your Batman ring," said Calvin.

"No way," I said. "I'm taking that with me."

I twisted the beautiful ring on my finger. I know Calvin's been eyeing my ring and wishing it were his. But it's not. It's mine. And at night, I always have to make sure that Calvin is in stage four deep sleep, with no eye movement or muscle activity, before I close my eyes, just in case.

"Fine, I don't really want it anyway," said Calvin.

But he did. I knew he wanted it real bad.

So I kept an eye on him until his eyes closed and his snoring began. If there is anything good about Calvin, it is this: He can never beat me in staying up late. I am often up with my flashlight, reading or making lists, because I'm afraid of the dark. But not Calvin. Calvin falls asleep just like that.

I watched his blanket go up and down.

Then I finished my Last Will and Testament:

And to my mom, I leave all my love.

I closed my eyes.
I thought of my mom.
I smelled her hair.
I hugged her neck.
I pressed my face against hers.
Then I cried myself to sleep.

CHAPTER TWELVE

The Scariest Morning of My Life

my dad is a great packer-upper. He packed Louise, his wasabi-green car, in no time. It is one of his talents.

But it is not one of mine. I wasn't packed at all.

"Son," said my dad. Usually, I like it when he calls me that. But this was not usual. It was the scariest morning of my life!

"It's time to go," said my dad.

I couldn't move. I couldn't speak. I was a won-ton in a wrapper.

But Anibelly wasn't. She was up and about and wide awake. She had on her Thunder Bunny backpack.

"Alvin isn't packed! Alvin isn't packed!" she squealed, hopping up and down and doing a little dance. "But I am!" she cried. "I'm packed!"

Anibelly took off her backpack. She un-zipped it. Thunder Bunny underwear fell out, and inside were a toothbrush, pieces of soap, Old Maid cards, a first-aid kit, a roll of toilet paper and a bunch of my supplies that came in Next Day Delivery. Hanging from the outside of the bag was a strange device.

"What's this?" asked my dad, inspecting the gadget.

"An eleven-in-one," said Anibelly.

"A what?"

"A mirror, fork, knife, spoon, thermometer, compass, whistle, flashlight, magnifying glass, hairbrush and weapon!" Anibelly said proudly. "I made it all by myself!" She had tied everything around one of my carved sticks, which looked like it was the weapon.

"Uncle Dennis told me about 'em," said Anibelly. "Secret Trick Number Two Hundred and Eighty-four!"

"That's fantastic!" said my dad, turning the thing around in his hands.

"So can I come too?" she asked.

My dad looked at Anibelly. Then he got down on his knees. "Sweetheart," he said, taking ahold of Anibelly's hand. "I promised Alvin that this would be a special time just with him."

The corners of Anibelly's lips wilted.

"But he's scared of camping!" Anibelly blurted. "He doesn't want to go. Take me instead!"

Why didn't I think of that? If Anibelly went, I wouldn't have to!

My dad blinked. "I'm not sure that's such a

good idea," he said slowly. "Why don't we plan on taking you *next* year, when you're . . . bigger?"

"I may be little, but I'm Anibelly Ho, Ready to Go!" said Anibelly. She stuck out her Hokey Pokey toe.

When it comes to Anibelly, my dad is squishy mochi cake. So I held my breath and shut my eyes and wished with all my might that Anibelly would get to go and I would get to stay home.

"Let's ask Alvin and see what he thinks," my dad said. "Alvin?"

"If you take her instead of me, you'll have a better time, Dad!" I blurted.

My dad looked over the tops of his glasses at me. He scratched his quillery cheek, then rubbed his quillery chin. It was not a good sign.

I had a sinking feeling.

"Well . . . ," said my dad. "If you really want to rough it in the woods, Anibelly, and you're packed, then of course you can come. You don't take up much room in the car . . . and we can squeeze you into our tent. We'd love to have you along."

Gulp.

"*We* would?" I asked. "You mean *I'm* going too?"

•●•●•

Packing like a maniac in three minutes flat was not a good idea.

I'm sure I forgot a bunch of stuff.

"It's only the Berkshires," said my dad. "We're not doing the Himalayas."

"Are you going to be okay, sweetheart?" asked my mom.

I breathed heavily through my N95 mask. I was not okay.

But I climbed into the car with Anibelly. Maybe it was a good thing Anibelly was coming along. She's not much, but she always makes me feel less scared. I don't know how she does it. Besides, having a buddy along for the buddy system is always a good idea. She might come in handy as an extra person to stand between me and the bears.

The bad thing about having Anibelly along was this: She doesn't take up much room in the car, she takes up ALL the room in the car. She may be little, but her car seat is HUGE. So there was hardly any room left for me!

The second bad thing about having Anibelly along was this: She sings.

"Lalalalalalalalala," she sang as we drove out of civilization and into the wilderness. "Lalalala-lalalalalalalalala."

It should have been a time of dread and planning ahead for disaster. But instead, it was a time of singing.

"Wanna learn a campfire song?" asked my dad. "It's one that we used to sing around the fires when the earth was still cooling."

"Yes!" cried Anibelly, kicking her legs.

"Okay, here it goes," said my dad. He sang:

"Let me tell you a story of a Scout named
    Anibelly.
On that tragic and fateful day,
Put her Scout knife in her pocket;
Kissed her dog and family;
Went to hike in the woods far away.
Well, did she ever return?
No, she never returned."

"Lalalalalalalalala," sang Anibelly.

"And her fate is still unlearned.
She may roam forever in the woods and
    mountains—
She's the Scout who never returned."

"Lalalalalalalala," sang Anibelly.

"*Waaaaaaaaaaaaaaaaaaaaaaaah,*" I cried as they sang. "*Waaaaaaaaaaaaaaaaaaaaaaaah.*"

"It's just a song, son," said my dad, looking at me in the mirror. "It's not for real, it's for *fun.*"

I nodded. I sniffed. I felt carsick.

My dad continued:

"*Now, you citizens of Concord,*
"*Don't you think it's a scandal,*

How ol' Anibelly got lost that day?
Take the right equipment;
TAKE ALONG A BUDDY,
When you hike in the hills that way.
Or else you'll never return,
No, you'll never return.
And your fate will be unlearned . . . Anibelly.
You may roam forever in the woods and
  mountains,
Like the Scout who never returned."

"*Ohhhhhhhhhhhhhhhhhhhhhhhhhhhhhh,*" I groaned as we drove closer and closer to the place of bears and rain and wild things, where flashlights don't work and matches won't strike, and from where—gulp—Scouts never return, which means they don't come back—dead or alive!

Fortunately, my dad didn't know any more words to the song and Anibelly soon fell asleep. It is one of her main talents, next to singing and to digging holes in the yard with my sticks. Anibelly can fall asleep just like that.

Anibelly has all the luck. If I could have

closed my eyes and not seen where we were going, I would have. But my eyes were stuck wide open just like binoculars.

It was quiet except for the sound of Louise charging full speed ahead.

I turned my Batman ring.

I looked out the window.

We were going so fast, the road beneath us didn't look like a road at all, it looked like the TV screen between channels. I felt thunder in my stomach and a rock in my shoe.

So I looked up. In the distance, the sky had turned a greenish blue with swirly clouds. The hillsides had a certain glow.

I recognized it:

"Tornadoes," I whispered. But no sound came out of my mouth.

CHAPTER THIRTEEN

Where's the Fried Rice?

this is how to know you are in trouble:

It smells like earthworms.

Rain grenades explode on your car.

Lightning splits the sky.

Thunder rumbles like a gigantic stomach.

Hubcaps roll by without cars.

This is how to know you are in grave danger:

Anibelly wakes up.

Then . . . "We interrupt this program for an emergency weather report. . . ." *Sssssssssssssssssssssss.*

There is only static on your radio.

And a chicken by the side of the road, being de-feathered by the wind.

"Hang on, kids," my dad screamed over the roar outside. He pulled over and turned off the engine.

Crrrraaaaaa-aaaaaaaaaaaa-aack! Everything turned baseball white.

Rrrrrrrrrrrrrrrrr-rrrrrrrmmmmmmmmm, rolled the thunder.

"Looks like a very bad thunderstorm," said my dad.

Thunderstorm? Traveling in a thunderstorm is extremely dangerous. The safest place is in a car, but we weren't safe at all, anyone could see that.

If we didn't get electrocuted, we could get drowned!

It was pouring like a faucet!

I turned my Batman ring.

Zzzzzzzzzzzzzzzzt! Lightning zapped the road in front of us.

Rrrrrrrrrrrrrrrrrrrrrmmmmmmmmmmm, the thunder rolled again.

So I turned my Batman ring again.

This time, lightning flashed in the distance and the thunder rolled farther away.

I turned my Batman ring one more time . . . and held my breath.

Soon the rain felt like drops from a lawn sprinkler.

"Is it over?" I asked.

"Maybe," said my dad. "Or maybe this is just the eye of the storm, where it's quiet before it starts again."

Eye of the storm? What could be creepier than that?

I turned my Batman ring like crazy.

My dad started the car.

My Batman ring had the secret power to make lightning and thunder go away.

Wow.

And now it was helping us get away from the creepy eye of the storm. Whatever that was.

.•.•.•.

By the time we got to the camping place, everything was very calm. The sun was shining. Louise rolled right into the parking lot. And we walked right onto our campsite. It smelled like a million pine trees.

"Setting up camp is the first order of business," said my dad. "Then we'll go on our first hike. How does that sound, kids?"

Silence.

Anibelly and I did not answer. We were doing "S" in the survival rules—sizing up the situation. It was not nighttime yet, but it was darker in the woods than in the parking lot, so I had slipped on my night-vision goggles and my N95 mask, just in case. And Anibelly had her weapon ready. We looked all around.

"Alvin, you will be the Keeper of the Flame,"

my dad announced. "Make sure that we have enough wood to burn. Keep our matches in a dry place. Do you think you can handle that?"

I nodded.

"Anibelly, you will be the Keeper of the Food," said my dad. "Make sure that our food is covered and put away at all times. Do you think you can handle that?"

Anibelly nodded.

"And I am the Keeper of All of Us," said my dad. "I will keep us safe at all times. Do you think I can handle that?"

"No," said Anibelly.

"Why not?" asked my dad.

"Because I'm hungry," said Anibelly. She put down her weapon. When Anibelly is hungry, she comes to a dead stop like a windup toy that has run out of windup.

"I'm starving too," I said. "In fact, I'm so hungry I could pass out right now immediately."

"Not a problem," said my dad. "Your mom packed us some fried rice. It's here somewhere. . . ."

"I can smell it," said Anibelly as my dad began taking things out of the bags he had carried in.

"Me too," I said. "I can smell it too." It was not a good sign. Starving men can always smell their favorite food before they die, I'm sure of it.

My dad took out a lot of things. In fact, he took out everything: a skillet, a little stove, canned beans, coffee beans, plates, forks, knives and spoons. But there was no fried rice. Not one little grain.

Silence.

"I must have forgotten it," my dad finally said. "Looks like I might have left an entire bag of food behind."

Silence.

"No problem!" said my dad. "I'll just open a can of beans and warm it on the stove and we'll have beans for lunch. There's nothing like eating beans right out of the can. No sirrreee. It's one of the highlights of camping."

Wow! Eating beans out of a can sounded terrific!

There was only one problem.

There was no can opener . . . anywhere.

"I must have left that at home too," said my dad.

Oops.

Soon we'd have to eat maggots and drink our own pee just as Uncle Dennis had said, I was sure of it. And that's when I saw it—the Angel of Death. It wasn't an angel exactly, but it was close enough. It was—gasp—an ALIEN from outer space! It was standing between some trees. It was SO ugly!

Then it began coming closer . . . and closer! It was coming straight for me! And when it got right up to me, it stopped. It smelled like Italian sandwiches, with the works. When I looked down, I saw that the alien's pockets were bulging with—Italian sandwiches! I drooled, just a little.

"Hello," said a man's voice. The alien had brought his kidnapped human dad with him.

"Hello," said my dad.

"We saw you folks arrive and thought we'd come over to welcome you," said the kidnapped human dad. "Your kids camping for the first time?"

"Yup," said my dad.

"My son's first time too," said the kidnapped human dad.

"Beaufeuillet, why don't you take off your gear and say hello," said the human to the alien.

"Howdy," said the alien. His antennae eyes

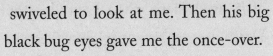

swiveled to look at me. Then his big black bug eyes gave me the once-over.

I said nothing. I don't talk to quadruple-eyed aliens.

"I'm Beaufeuillet," said the alien. "Boo-few-LAY the Fourth. My dad is Beaufeuillet the Third."

Beaufeuillet? If ever there was an alien name, that sure was it. And if ever I wished I had my Alien Destroyer Ultimate Decimator, it was then. But I'd forgotten to pack it.

Beaufeuillet slid off his bug eyes—they were not bug eyes, but a pair of night-vision goggles, just like mine! He was not an alien at all; he was a boy, just like me. And he was about my size except that he was so skinny he looked like a cricket.

"I sure wasn't counting on meeting a real live alien," said Beaufeuillet, "until I saw your head poking through the woods. Then I stopped dead in my tracks, and I said, 'That is an alien from outer space!' You scared the dead night-light out of me, popped my belly button right off!"

Anibelly's eyes popped out like golf balls. She stared him smack in the eyes, then she stared at his pockets. She swallowed. "I'm Anibelly Ho," said Anibelly. "And that's Alvin. He's not an alien. He's my brother. And he doesn't talk to strangers."

Beaufeuillet swiveled all his eyes at me. "Okay," he said, shrugging. "Want a sandwich?" He reached into his bulging pockets.

"We had extras," said Beaufeuillet's dad. "We thought you might be hungry after your drive."

"You have no idea," said my dad, taking the sandwiches. "Thanks very much."

"We're in the high-tech foil tent," said Beaufeuillet's dad, pointing at something in the distance that looked like it could be—gasp—a UFO! "Come by anytime."

Then Beaufeuillet snapped his night-vision

goggles back into place. "You like superheroes?" he asked.

I nodded.

"Ever hear of Night Vision Man?"

I shook my head no.

"Well, I am he!" he said, giving his chest a thump.

"Come along, son," said his dad.

"Coming, Dad."

But for a minute, Night Vision Man didn't go anywhere. He stood right where he was and peered at me through his many eyes.

"Do you like camping?" he asked.

I shook my head.

"Neither do I," he whispered. "We could die out here, you know."

I knew.

"Well, see you!" he said. Then he ran to catch up with his human dad.

And I sat down with mine and we ate yummy Italian sandwiches together with Anibelly.

And that was how we got saved from starving to death before the scary camping even got started.

CHAPTER FOURTEEN

Avoid Disturbing Your Environment

this is how to pitch a tent.

1. Find a good spot. Not too high (too windy). Not too low (too wet).
2. Unfold your tent.

3. Pound some stakes into the ground.
4. Follow the directions that came with the tent.
5. Make some hot chocolate.
6. Drink the hot chocolate.

7. Reread the directions.

8. Pull the stakes out of the ground.

9. Move them around.

10. Pound them in again.

11. Try to remember how you did it two hundred years ago when tents didn't come with directions and you could put one up anyway.

12. Scratch your head.

13. Rub your chin.

14. Walk away and work on digging a pit toilet for a while.

15. Dig hard and fast because your kids are crying that they'd rather die than use a pit toilet and Anibelly is walking off with

some of the tent stuff and doing her own thing.

16. Repeat steps 3 through 16 until your tent is standing without your kids holding it up.
17. Stand back and admire.
18. Go in and check it out!

19. Don't panic.

20. Find your way out of the collapsed tent.

21. Repeat.

When our tent was finally up for good, my dad looked pretty beat. In fact, he looked a lot like Calvin's very old bunny with the stuffing coming out.

"I sure could use a nap," he said, diving head-first into the tent.

This was good news. It meant that we didn't have to go on a scary hike up a scary mountain. Hooray!

But it was also bad news.

"Dad?" I shoved my dad a couple of times. He was safely tucked inside his sleeping bag, snoring. And Anibelly and I were not safely

tucked anywhere. "Wake up, Dad!" I cried. "If you snooze, we . . . lose."

"Rrrrrrrrr," growled my dad. *"Rrrrrrrrrr."*

That's the problem with my dad. Once he falls asleep, he's as hard to get started as a dead car battery.

Anibelly and I were in trouble now.

The Keeper of the Fire had no fire to keep.

The Keeper of the Food had no food to guard.

And the Keeper of All of Us was out—like a rocket into outer space.

Gulp.

"Anibelly," I said. "I think this means that *I'm* now the Keeper of All of Us."

"Yup," said Anibelly. "Let's build traps."

"How are traps going to help us?"

"Secret Trick Number Four Hundred and Fifty-two," said Anibelly. "Traps catch monsters and bears. Just when they're about to grab you— oops—they'll trip and dangle, just like that!"

It sounded good to me. Plus, Anibelly was amazing at remembering Uncle Dennis's How-to-Make-a-Trap instructions:

"First, don't disturb nature," said Anibelly. We tiptoed around our campsite, especially around our tent where my dad was sleeping.

"Second, wash your hands," said Anibelly. We rubbed dirt and sand on our hands.

"Whatcha doin'?" said a voice. It was Beaufeuillet. His extra eyes were rolling around.

"Making traps," I said.

"Want some help?" asked Beaufeuillet.

"Can you tie triple knots?" I said, unpacking the ropes and rubber cords that my dad had packed.

"Sure!" said Beaufeuillet. "My dad's taught me all sorts of knots and traps. Square . . . overhand . . . fisherman's . . . and as for the traps: mangle, tangle, dangle and strangle."

I stopped. He knew them all, just like my uncle Dennis! "Okay, you can help," I told him.

First, we showed Beaufeuillet how to tie a sapling and make it bend. Then Beaufeuillet

showed us how to make a snare for something heavy by throwing a cord over a branch of a regular-sized tree and setting it in a spring between two branches in the ground.

Then we made more traps. After that, we covered our traps with mud and leaves and moss.

"Check your traps often," I said, finally remembering one of the rules of trap making. "It's important to not let anyone be surprised for too long."

We sized up the situation. There were SO many traps around our camp, but you would never know it. You couldn't see a single one. Uncle Dennis would be proud. Best of all, I felt a little safer and so did Anibelly.

Until . . . I remembered something.

"Don't traps need bait?" I asked.

"Sure do," said Beaufeuillet. "When I go fishing with my dad, we always use bait—without it, the fish won't bite. He's looking for bait now so that we can go fishing."

"Bait?" said Anibelly. "What's bait?"

"It's the little thing used to catch something bigger," I said.

"BOOO-FEW-LAY," a voice called through the woods. "Time to go!"

"There's my dad," said Beaufeuillet. "He must have found our bait. Gotta run." Then he was gone.

And Anibelly and I were left alone with our traps.

We looked around at all the traps that we could not see.

We used all our senses.

Just when I'd about figured it out, Anibelly gasped. How she ever figured it out before I did, I'll never know.

"*We* are the bait," she whispered.

CHAPTER FIFTEEN

What Would Calvin Do?

anibelly sprang like a rabbit from a snare.

"I may be bait," she shrieked, "but I'm still Anibelly Ho and I'm not sitting bait, I'm fighting bait!

"C'mon, Alvin, we gotta move fast!"

Anibelly ran toward the car, and I ran after her.

"Hurry, Alvin," said Anibelly, crawling into the back of Louise. "We gotta get our stuff and use it to protect ourselves!"

In the back, underneath an old blanket, was

the portable diesel generator, the Monster Eye flashlight, mosquito netting and the rest of the stuff that Calvin had ordered.

"Calvin helped me hide this stuff in here last night," said Anibelly. "Just in case."

If there was anything good about having Anibelly along, it was this: She's a fantastic packer-upper.

"Aren't you glad I came?" asked Anibelly.

I nodded. "You're very useful, Anibelly," I said. It sounded like something Calvin would say to her. He always has a good word for Anibelly, but I hardly ever do on account of it's hard to be nice to a girl.

Then Anibelly stopped. "Now what?" she asked. She looked at the equipment, and then she looked at me.

"Now we . . . we . . ." I scratched my head. I didn't know what we were going to do. Calvin had ordered everything without explaining anything.

"What would Calvin do?" asked Anibelly.

"He would test all the equipment to make

sure everything works," I said. "That's what Calvin would do."

"Okay!" said Anibelly. She was a regular professional tester. Often Calvin and I would ask her to be the first to try something to see if it was dangerous, or poisonous or something. And she would do it and report the facts, exactly as they were.

So we climbed out of the car and dumped everything out of its box and gave it all a trial run.

Everything was okay . . . except for the generator, which wouldn't start, and the mosquito netting, which was so tangled and heavy that you could hardly see or breathe through it . . . we needed scissors, but Calvin didn't order scissors, so we tried bushwhacking our way out with the Monster Eye flashlight, but it was not a good machete at all. So then I asked,

"What would Houdini do?"

"Squirm!" cried Anibelly. So we squirmed like crazy. It was great! But we were even more tangled than before.

Finally Anibelly unzipped the mosquito netting and slipped out, just like that.

Mosquito netting sure works up an appetite, so we tore into the energy bars, which was a wonderful idea, except that they were kind of gooey.

And they got stuck in our throats.

So then we purified a puddle right there in the parking lot, on account of we needed to wash down the sticky morsels quickly before we choked to death.

The water-purification tablets worked great!

But we still couldn't figure out how to get the generator going so we could protect ourselves by running the portable TV, which Calvin had also packed. As everyone knows, having the TV on can keep coyotes away.

"I know what Calvin would do," said Anibelly. "Take it apart!" My brother Calvin can figure out anything just by taking it apart and putting it back together. It's the first thing he does with a new toy and it always teaches him a thing or two about how things work.

So Anibelly and I took the generator apart.

Then we put it back together.

When we were done, there were only a handful of tiny thingies that didn't belong anywhere.

The portable diesel generator looked almost exactly the same as when it came out of the box.

But it still didn't work. So there was only one thing left to do. . . .

"Let's take the Monster Eye apart to see what makes it so bright!" I said.

"Okay!" said Anibelly.

So then we took apart our flashlight.

And we put it back together.

After that, our very fantastic Monster Eye Wide beam wasn't so bright anymore. In fact, you could say it was rather dark.

"That's a rip-off," I said. "Calvin said that for four hundred dollars it should shine forever!"

I was really disappointed.

And scared. We had *nothing* to protect ourselves.

But Anibelly didn't notice.

"Camping is really fun, isn't it, Alvin?" she asked.

I stopped.

I looked at Anibelly.

Anibelly was looking at me and smiling like the crinkly top of one of my mom's apple pies. She was so happy, she couldn't sing. She couldn't even be chatty. She was just kind of there, floating above the colorful autumn leaves in the golden afternoon light. You might even say that she was *glowing*.

"I wish that we could stay here and camp forever!" said Anibelly, hugging herself.

Then Anibelly wrapped her noodle arms around me. She breathed softly, her eyes closed.

So I closed my eyes. I sighed. Maybe I was enjoying camping a little too . . . and just as I was about to tell her that . . .

A loud WHOOOOOOOOOOOOOOOSH went over the tops of the trees. . . .

Then a belly-button-piercing scream shook the entire forest.

CHAPTER SIXTEEN

Not a Happy Camper

"**aaaaaaaaaaaaaaaaack!!!!**"

Silence.

"AAAAAAAAAAAAAAAALVIN HOOOOOOOOOOOOOO!!!!"

Uh-oh.

Anibelly and I had forgotten to check our traps. We ran over to them.

"Swim with leeches!" my dad screamed. He was dangling upside down by one leg and his whole body was twisting like crazy, just like Houdini in the Great Upside-Down Escape!

"Thou bootless guts-gripping bum-bailey better have an explanation for this, or sorrow on thee! I'll not be a mangled swag-bellied death token." My dad was not a happy camper. And when my dad is not a happy camper, watch out—he will curse like Shakespeare.

"But it's not a mangle trap," I tried to explain. "It's a dangle one."

"WE'RE CAMPING, NOT HUNTING AND TRAPPING!" said my dad. He was very pink, almost red. Normally, he is neither.

"Hey, Dad," said Anibelly. "You look like a great big piñata!"

"You're definitely the biggest, fattest piñata I've ever seen!" I added.

Oops.

"I mean, you look great, Dad," I said. "You'd definitely be a hit at a party."

"Ohhhhhhhhhhhh," said my dad. He stopped twisting. And when piñatas stop swinging, they start spinning.

"Aaaaaaaaaaaaaaaaaaaaaaaaaiiiiiii," cried my dad. He went round and round.

"Uncle Dennis taught us real good traps, didn't he, Dad?" asked Anibelly.

"Uncle Dennis?" my dad began. "Why, that incurable mad-brained clack-dish!"

I held my breath.

I opened my ears.

This is when the truth comes out. Whenever someone on TV is dangling upside down and being knocked about like a human piñata, secrets spill from their mouths like coins from their pockets.

I leaned closer. My dad was about to tell me that my uncle Dennis was a secret agent, I was sure of it.

"I'll see thee hang'd, thou spongy weather-

bitten jolthead!" cried my dad. Then he *really* cried, real tears, upside down.

•·•·•·

Setting traps sure was fun.

But setting my dad free was not. I really wanted to help him, but I couldn't. I am acrophobic. So I ran into our tent and I slipped on my Firecracker Man outfit and ran back.

But Firecracker Man is acrophobic too, I forgot.

So how he ever got up in the tree, I'll never know.

"Go, Alvin!" screamed Anibelly. "You can do it!"

"NOOOOOO!" I wanted to scream back, but I couldn't scream. I was draped over a branch like a scallion pancake and hanging on for dear life.

"Just a little farther!" cried Anibelly.

"C'mon, son," said my dad. "You're the Keeper of All of Us now. You can do it."

The wind picked up. Birds gossiped. I was completely freaked out.

"It's getting dark, son," said my dad. "It would be better if you moved just a little faster."

Dark? No problem! With my night-vision goggles, I'll never be afraid of the dark again!

Too bad my night-vision goggles were in the car.

"*Waaaaaaaaaaaaaaaaaaaaaaaaaaah!*"

I hugged the branch and cried my eyes out. After that, I felt much better. But I still couldn't move very fast. In fact, I don't think I moved at all.

"Whatcha up to?" came

Beaufeuillet's voice. He was breathless and his eyes were bouncing and rolling around like crazy, taking everything in. "I was down at the lake when I heard a loud scream."

"It's our dad!" cried Anibelly. "He stepped into one of our traps!"

"Time for Night Vision Man!" said Beaufeuillet. He lowered his night-vision goggles onto his eyes and thumped himself on the chest.

"Hooray!" said Anibelly.

But Night Vision Man did not move.

"What's the matter, son?" asked my dad. "Can you go up and give my son a hand?"

Silence.

It was not a good sign.

"No, sir," Beaufeuillet began, "I've never climbed a tree before in my life. I'm . . . I'm . . . scared of heights!"

So how Night Vision Man ever got up in the tree, I'll never know. But there he was, trembling and wailing and hanging on for dear life right next to me! Then suddenly, he was quiet. He reached out and grabbed my ankle, firmly.

"Gotcha," he said. "Night Vision Man . . . won't let you fall . . . no matter what."

Slowly I slid out on the branch. A millimeter took a LONG, LONG, LOOOONG time.

When I finally got to where I needed to be, it got even scarier.

First I had to take my dad's Scout knife out of my pocket.

Then I had to pry it open.

Then I had to start sawing away at the rubber cord. I had to cut through it so that my dad could fall to the ground.

"Don't drop the knife, Alvin!" cried Anibelly.

"Don't fall out of the tree, Alvin!

"Don't give up, Alvin!"

Anibelly was trying to be helpful. But she really was not. She was on the ground. And I was up in the tree.

"But it's okay to cry, Alvin!" said Anibelly. "One wrong move and you're going to be dead anyway!"

Gulp.

I could see the cord ripping now . . . it was almost there.

"Don't look down, Alvin!" Anibelly shrieked.

"Don't even *think* of looking down!"

My dad was now swinging by a thin rubber thread. . . .

"But if you do look," cried Anibelly, "and you fall . . . Mom always says—"

Fwap!

Anibelly stopped. My dad was hurtling headfirst like a torpedo toward Earth. But if anyone can remember advice in a hurry and repeat it, it's Anibelly.

"TRY TO LAND ON YOUR BUTT!"

CHAPTER SEVENTEEN

Facing the Stars

after my dad fell with a thump to the ground, he rescued Firecracker Man and Night Vision Man from the tree, even before brushing himself off.

"Your uncle Dennis is SO busted," my dad mumbled. Then he inspected us for night-vision loss, jelly knee syndrome, permanent bonelessness, missing fingers, missing teeth and general irreversible damage.

We had a few scrapes, but we were okay.

"Traps are dangerous," said my dad. "Promise you won't build any more."

"Promise," I said.

"Promise," said Beaufeuillet.

"Okay," said Anibelly.

Then it was time to build a fire. Thanks to our collection of dryer lint, Anibelly and I helped get our campfire started right away. My dad was very impressed. So we didn't tell him that it was Uncle Dennis's Secret Trick No. 1.

After that, Beaufeuillet's dad returned with the day's catch and cooked it over our fire and shared it with us. He wasn't any good at starting a fire, he said, but he was good at fishing and they had more food than they could eat. They also had a can opener, so we had canned beans too. And there was corn on the cob and kettle cake, which you bake in the hot coals. It was a feast!

We ate and ate. Our dads talked about fishing and camping and hiking. And we talked about our very exciting afternoon with the traps and how Firecracker Man and Night Vision Man had come to the rescue.

After that, it got really dark.

I saw faces in the fire.

And faces in the trees.

Stars winked through the sky's dark blanket.

It got really creepy.

Anibelly grabbed her weapon.

"It's time for a ceremony," said my dad, moving next to the fire.

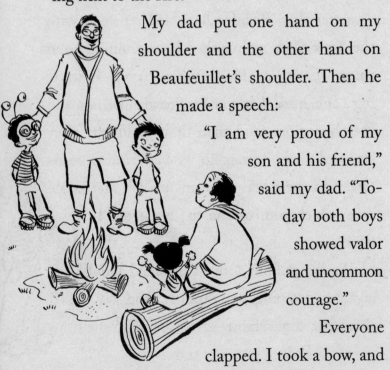

My dad put one hand on my shoulder and the other hand on Beaufeuillet's shoulder. Then he made a speech:

"I am very proud of my son and his friend," said my dad. "Today both boys showed valor and uncommon courage."

Everyone clapped. I took a bow, and

so did Beaufeuillet. Then my dad got down on his knees and looked us smack in our night-vision goggles.

"You two are the true Keepers of All of Us," he said. "From your daring performance today, I know that you would never let any harm come to those you love."

"But I cried a lot and I was scared to death!" I said.

"And I almost didn't make it up the tree," said Beaufeuillet.

"A hero is someone who is willing to be scared," said Beaufeuillet's dad.

"*Super-duper* scared," added Anibelly.

"So here, now . . . in front of a reliable eye-witness, Miss Anibelly, and in the great assembly of trees, we now pronounce each of you to be Keepers of All of Us," said my dad.

"Amen!" yelled Anibelly. Then she stepped forward and tapped me, and then Beaufeuillet, on the shoulders with her weapon.

"How does it feel?" asked Anibelly.

"Fantastic!" said Beaufeuillet.

"Great!" I said. "But you deserve to be changed too, Anibelly."

"Really?" said Anibelly. "What did I do?"

"You told me not to quit," I said.

So then I took Anibelly's weapon and tapped her on the shoulders.

"I hereby pronounce you Most Valuable Player of the Year," I said. "MVP, make no mistake about it."

"Wow," said Anibelly. "I thought only baseball players got that."

"Well, you play baseball, don't you?"

"Yup," said Anibelly. "I play it very well."

"Well, then, that settles that," I said.

Then Beaufeuillet looked at me. And I looked at him.

"We're real superheroes," he said.

"Dude," I said.

"Dude."

•-•-•-•

After that, we sang some campfire songs, but not the scary ones.

My dad sang:

"I waaaaaant—to awaken to sky and fat little
birdies singing in the trees!
I waaaaaaaant—to sit by a blaze and toast my
toes and roast some marshmallows while the
crickets serenade!
Oh yeah, baby, I'll do all this and more—
Because I am camping outdoor!"

My dad sang the loudest and Anibelly sang the second loudest and Beaufeuillet's dad sang pretty loud too. But Beaufeuillet and I sang barely above a whisper so as not to attract too much attention from whatever was out there watching us.

Then it was time for bed.

The Beaufeuillets went home to their tent.

And we went into ours.

It was the perfect ending to a scary day.

Until . . . we needed to use the toilet.

My dad and his flashlight started to head downhill toward the pit.

Anibelly and I and our very dim Monster Eye Narrow Beam flashlight did not.

"Aren't you guys coming?" he asked.

"No," said Anibelly.

"Well, why not?" asked my dad.

"Because I left my toilet paper in the normal bathroom," said Anibelly.

"You don't need toilet paper," said my dad.

"Yes, I do," said Anibelly. She stuck out her hiking-booted toe.

"Out here, Nature gives you plenty of toilet paper," said my dad. "Besides, using leaves is better for the environment."

Coals sizzled in the fire.

"No thanks," said Anibelly. "Alvin and I are going to the normal bathroom, aren't we, Alvin?"

We are? In the dark? By ourselves?

Fortunately, my dad is tofu jelly when it comes to Anibelly. So he walked us over to the building that said "Toilets," and he walked us back to camp before going down to the pit by himself.

When my dad got back—surprise, surprise—he was okay!

"Could we sleep out under the stars tonight?" I asked.

"You want to sleep *out*?"

I nodded.

"Me too," said Anibelly.

"You're not scared?" asked my dad.

"I'm so scared I could pee in my pants," I said. "But I've used the bathroom, and now I want to see the stars."

So then we bundled into our sleeping bags and slept out. It was cold, but it was okay. And this is what we saw:

The North Star.

The Big Dipper.

Cassiopeia.

Orion's Belt.

And the Milky Way, which is not milky at all, but a silver river of a million stars, that looked just like—my mom when she's dressed up all special!

It was the most beautiful thing I'd ever seen.

"Did you know," my dad began, "Henry David Thoreau said that one of his first memories was staying awake at night 'looking through the stars to see if I could see God behind them'?"

So I did what Henry did. I looked for God. Then I poked Anibelly so that she could look too.

But Anibelly's eyes were closed. Her face, lit by the sprinkles falling from a million stars, looked like the top of a birthday cake lit by candles. She was fast asleep.

"Have you ever seen any UFOs, Dad?" I whispered. I thrust an arm into the cold air and reached to hold my dad's hand.

"I don't think so," said my dad. "But I

remember wishing for a whole fleet of them to fly over my head."

"How about aliens?"

"No," said my dad. "No luck there either."

"Were you always so brave, Dad?"

"No," said my dad. "Not always. I used to be afraid of everything."

"Like me?"

"Yes, like you."

"Did you always like camping?" I asked.

"Yes," said my dad. "Always."

"What did you like about it?"

"Everything," he said. "But especially this— falling asleep facing the stars."

"Me too," I said. "I'm just like you, Dad."

My dad squeezed my hand. And I squeezed him back.

"I love you, son."

"I love you, Dad."

Then I closed my eyes and went to sleep.

CHAPTER EIGHTEEN

Never Put All Your Toilet Paper in One Place

the crack of dawn isn't what it's cracked up to be.

I was waiting for the sky to crack open like a big walnut and for the sun to come shining through.

It didn't. There wasn't an explosion, or even a loud *crack* to announce the new day. I was really disappointed. Instead, this is what happens: The light begins gradually, silently, you don't even really notice it, until you say hey, it's not night-time anymore, and pop out of your sleeping bag!

After a breakfast of eggs and hash brown potatoes cooked over the fire, Anibelly and I were ready for another day of scary camping.

"How 'bout a hike?" asked my dad.

I was ready. I had my hiking stick. I had my trauma kit. I had my water-purification tablets. I had my N95 mask. I had my mirror and GPS. But I was missing something . . . I couldn't quite put my finger on it . . . what was it?

"We'll take my little portable stove with us and make hot chocolate at the top of the moun-tain where there's a view," said my dad.

The *top* of the mountain?

"We can make hot chocolate fine right here," I said.

"From the top, we'll see the beautiful New England foliage for miles," said my dad.

"I can see it fine from here," I said. It was true. The beautiful leaves were all around us, even under our feet. Orange-, cinnamon-, butter-, and burnt-toast-colored, the leaves looked like fireworks. There was nothing but beautiful New England foliage between our tent and our car.

Then my dad moved some rocks into an arrow pointing into the trees.

"What's that for?" I asked.

"It's a direction marker," said my dad. "It tells rescuers which way we went."

Gulp. "We'll need rescuing?"

"I hope not," said my dad. "But experienced campers and hikers always leave signs, just in case."

I froze.

"C'mon, Alvin," said Anibelly. I've got the toilet paper, so we'll be okay."

What would Henry do? He would hike, I'm sure of it. And before I knew it, we were going through the jungle, where my dad showed us other signs.

"See the bird circling up there?" he asked. "If it's a hawk, it means there's prey below. If it's a turkey vulture, it means something's dead on the ground."

Crunch, crunch, crunch. Leaves crackled with every step.

"If you see squirrels hoarding nuts or a lot of rabbits during the day, it means bad weather is on the way. . . ."

"And you can smell rain coming," my dad said. "It smells like trees and flowers and grass because everything opens up to receive it." We sniffed the air.

"This is hiking, Dad?" asked Anibelly.

"Yup," said my dad, "this is hiking."

"But it's just walking and talking," said Anibelly. "I thought hiking was something else."

"I thought hiking was where you beat back the bushes with a sword and you get all sweaty and look like you're about to die," said Anibelly, who gets very chatty whenever she is happy and talks about anything that comes to mind. "Oh, how I wish I had a guinea pig!"

"Anibelly," I hissed, "as the new Keeper of All of Us, it's my job to inform you that you're attracting all sorts of attention with your loud talking. You're supposed to be quiet so you don't disturb your environment."

Anibelly stopped. She looked at me. "Okay," she whispered. "Oh, how I wish I had a guinea pig."

•–•–•

How we ever got to the top of the mountain, I'll never know. But we did. And it was beautiful, just as my dad had said. And we drank hot chocolate, just as he had promised.

A lot of other people were there too. Some were picnicking. Others were looking through their binoculars and checking their compasses. Some were even napping on the rocks! Imagine that! Napping on a slippery rock when you should be hanging on for dear life! A hawk circled nearby.

"Relax, son," said my dad. He clapped his hand on my shoulder. "Try to enjoy the view."

So I did. I looked out at the whole world exploding in foliage fireworks, which is the same view I get from the postcards in the candy store that were just as pretty and a lot less dangerous.

"It's always so peaceful here," said my dad. "People come for the peace and quiet."

Then my dad stretched out on a rock and closed his eyes.

It was not a good sign. What would Henry do if his dad fell asleep on him?

Henry would have his hiking stick. I had mine. I also had my trauma kit. I had my N95 mask. I had my sunscreen. I had my GPS and mirror. I had my Batman ring.

I stopped.

I checked my finger.

I *stared* at my finger.

My finger was naked!

My Batman ring was gone!

"Where's my Batman ring????" I could hardly say it.

My dad rolled over on the rock.

"I can't find my Batman ring," I said, a little louder.

Silence.

I checked my pockets.

"Where's my BATMAN RING?"

I checked my backpack.

"Has anyone seen my BATMAN RING???

"I CAN'T FIND MY BATMAN RING!!!!"

My dad sat up with a start.

"MY BATMAN RING IS GONE!" I hollered.

"Are you sure you brought it with you?" asked my dad.

"Yesssssssssssss!"

"Where did you last see it?"

"I don't *knoooooooooooooooooooooooooooooooow*!" I howled.

"MY BATMAN RING!!!!!" I screeched. "WHERE'S MY BATMAN RING???????"

More hawks circled nearby.

"Calm down," said my dad.

"I'LL DIE WITHOUT MY BAT-MAAAAAAN RIIIIIIING!!!!"

"Get him off the mountain," said a lady.

"You're disturbing the peace!" said a Boy Scout.

"WAAAAAAAAAAAAAAAAAAAAAAAAAH!"

"Go home!" someone shouted.

How we ever got down the mountain, I'll never know.

All I know is that my dad is very sympathetic. He had planned to take us fishing, but instead, he helped me look for my Batman ring. And when we got back to our campsite, Beaufeuillet and his extra eyes and his dad came over and helped too. We looked *all* afternoon.

But my Batman ring was nowhere to be found.

Worse, it was time to pack and go home.

"Bye," said Beaufeuillet. "I hope you find your ring."

"Thanks," I whispered, choking back tears.

We waved good-bye to the Beaufeuillets, and my dad finished packing, while Anibelly and I continued searching.

"I can't leave without my Batman ring!" I cried. "I need its secret powers!"

"You don't need secret powers," said my dad. "You were a great camper without it."

"Maybe it was the ring's secret powers that helped me rescue you yesterday!" I cried.

My dad scratched his head.

Then he scratched his backside, which is a polite word for his you-know-what.

Then he tugged on his shorts and scratched his backside some more.

"I don't remember seeing a ring on you," said my dad. "Are you *sure* you brought it?"

I nodded.

My dad took a deep breath.

Then he took another deep breath.

"Where did you ever find a Batman ring anyway?" he asked. "They made those things for only one year, when I was about your age."

"Uncle Dennis."

"Uncle Dennis???" My dad didn't sound too pleased. "Traps . . . secret powers . . . what other camping tips did your uncle Dennis give you?" he asked.

"Use toilet paper," said Anibelly. "And never put all your toilet paper in one place."

"Ohhhhhhhhhhhhhhhhhh," moaned my dad. Then he scratched his butt . . . like crazy!

"Are you okay, Dad?" asked Anibelly.

"Noooo," groaned my dad. "We gotta get home—fast!"

"NOOOOOOOOOOOOooooooooooooo!!!!" I howled. "My riiiiiiiing!"

But before I knew it, my dad had picked me up, put me in the car and belted me in, just like that. And Anibelly was safe in her car seat next to me.

I cried my eyes out as we sped toward

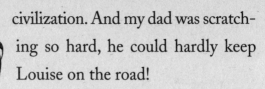

civilization. And my dad was scratching so hard, he could hardly keep Louise on the road!

Suddenly, my backside hurt. Uh-oh. Was I going to start scratching like my dad? I rolled to one side. Something was sticking to the butt of my pants, so I picked it off and held it up.

Anibelly gasped.

My Batman ring!

It had been in the car the whole time! I slipped the ring quickly back on my finger.

"Aren't you going to tell Dad?" whispered Anibelly.

"Tell Dad what?" growled my dad.

"Nothing," I peeped.

.•.•.

When we got home, my mom and Calvin were waiting for us with a yummy dinner of fried rice with everything in it. It smelled like home and tasted like Chinese New Year.

Anibelly filled her belly.

And so did I.

But my dad did not.

He was in the bathroom next to the kitchen, crying . . . and jumping up and down so that the whole house shook.

"Did you like camping?" asked my mom.

"It was okay," I said. "There was a thunderstorm. We ate Italian sandwiches. We looked at the stars. I made a new friend."

"It was great!" said Anibelly. "We sang a

camping song about me! Our new friends were both Boo-few-LAY."

"You met a couple of buffalo?" asked Calvin.

"No, that was their name," I said. "Boo-few-LAY. At first I thought he was an alien from outer space with a kidnapped human dad, but he turned out to be a superhero just like me!"

"How wonderful!" said my mom. "Speaking of friends, Flea is on her way over. She can't wait to hear about your trip."

.•.•.

It was great to tell Flea all about roughing it in the woods with my dad and Anibelly. It was a lot rougher than her camp for kids with disabilities, that's for sure. In fact, it was *so* rough, it made her jealous, I'm sure of it.

So I toned it down a little.

"We nearly starved to death," I said. "Then my dad got trapped and nearly dangled to death. Then he nearly scratched himself to death. And there was a deadly storm.

"I even saw the Angel of Death—but it was an alien."

"Alvin," said my mom, giving me the look. She was not impressed.

But Flea was. She was really impressed. She was so impressed, she didn't know what to say. She picked at her Fried Rice Special with chopsticks and nodded with her mouth open.

"But the alien turned out to be a kid just like me," I said, thumping myself on the chest. "And we became friends."

"So you weren't kidnapped?" Flea asked.

"Nope," I said. "Anibelly and I protected ourselves pretty well with the stuff Calvin helped me order on the Internet," I confessed.

"What stuff?" Flea wanted to know.

"A generator that didn't work and a big flashlight called the Monster Eye," said Anibelly.

Silence.

"You bought what?" came my dad's voice from the bathroom.

"A generator for disaster use

and a great big monster flashlight that didn't work after we took it apart!" Anibelly screamed through the bathroom door. "And a whole bunch of other stuff too!" she added.

My dad stopped crying.

"Ask Alvin how he paid for it," came a low growl.

"Alvin, how did you pay for it?" asked Anibelly.

"Calvin used Dad's emergency credit—"

"WHAAAAAAAAAAAAAAAAAAT?" screamed my dad from behind the closed door. "Oh nooooooooooooooooooooooo!"

I turned my Batman ring.

Then my dad burst out in the loudest sobbing I've ever heard in my entire life. Not only did he not have secret Bat-powers, but he had wiped his butt with the scariest thing of all— poison ivy.

My poor dad. If I could give him any good advice, it would be this: He really should have used toilet paper.

Alvin Ho's
Very Scary Glossary

acrophobia—Fear of being at the top of ladders, on the roof, or on any floor of a skyscraper higher than the second.

arachnophobia—Fear of creepy spiders!

Batman ring—(1) Black, (2) rubbery, (3) you have to turn it to release its secret powers.

camping—(1) must be done in the woods, (2) with all the right equipment, (3) aka "roughing it."

claustrophobia—Fear of small, tiny spaces that feel like they're going to squish the air right out of you, such as elevators, airplanes, closets, or the inside of a dishwasher-sized time machine.

eye of the storm—The center of the storm, which looks like a creepy eye in the sky.

geological age—A long, long time, at least 22 million years and as many as 79.2 million years, but not long enough to finish your homework.

GPS—Used to stand for Good old-fashioned Pointing Stick, but now it's a screen and it points you to where you need to go. If you can't read a compass, get a GPS.

gunggung—Chinese word for grandpop on your mom's side. He's super-duper!

Harry Houdini—Famous dead guy who was the best escape artist in the world! His real name was Erik Weisz. Comes in a kit now for everyday use. Made in China.

Henry David Thoreau—(1) Famous dead author and a mostly cool dude who liked the woods and camping with his dad. (2) He called himself Inspector of Snowstorms and Rainstorms. (3) His parents named him David Henry, but he switched to Henry David when he grew up. (4) Born and died in Concord, Massachusetts, which is hard to spell.

hiking—Walking through the woods in stiff boots while watching out for bears, snakes, coyotes and other wild animals that can kill you on account of you can't run very fast in those stiff boots.

kettle cake—One egg, one cup of water, half a cup of vegetable oil, stir with one box of cake mix in cast-iron kettle. Put lid on kettle. Put kettle in hot coals in the campfire. Wait. Check under the lid (remember to use an oven mitt!). Wait again. In fact, wait a geological age until it's bubbly, then use a spoon and dig in!

last will and testament—Is kind of like homework. (1) You think about all the things you own, (2) you think about all the people you love, (3) you match the people with the things. For example,

Anibelly—1 piece of sea glass
Calvin—old socks

This way the right people get the right things after you die. Sometimes this works, and sometimes it doesn't. When it doesn't, you have to take it with you, just as I'll take my Batman ring.

Mesozoic era—Back when Earth was cooling, but still warm as an oven! Mesozoic means "middle animals," which includes dinosaurs!

Meteorite—An extraterrestrial rock that lands on Earth. (1) Sometimes they're a hot fireball, (2) sometimes they cause a crater, (3) sometimes they strike a person dead.

N95 respirator mask—Looks like a white beak over your nose and mouth. (1) Double straps adjust to your head size, (2) stops germs and dust from getting in, (3) perfect for allergy protection while running around the yard like crazy or while camping, (4) made in China.

nyctophobia—Fear of the dark, especially at night . . . in a tent . . . with nothing between you and the coyotes but a zipper.

poison ivy—(1) A three-leafed plant that has an oil in its leaves, vines and roots that can make you look like a scary alien if you touch it or touch something that has touched it (like your clothes or dog), (2) scarier than chicken pox, (3) could last up to three itchy weeks.

portable generator—Looks like a heavy-duty ice chest for cold drinks, but is actually a giant battery that can power a TV to keep the coyotes away, if you can get it started.

secret agent—Everyone knows what a secret agent is.

Shakespeare—(1) Last name of William. (2) Dead English author. (3) Born after Christopher Columbus discovered the Americas, but died before the British Army wore red. (4) Wrote lots of plays, poems, curses, everything. When he ran out of words, he made up new ones. (5) Never lived in Concord.

tsunami—Pronounced "soo-NAH-mee." A bunch of scary waves from the ocean that look like one GIGANTIC wave or the Great Wall of China rushing ashore to eat you up alive.

water-purification tablets—Pills for making sick water healthy. Dissolve one pill in one quart of bad water. Caution: Do not swallow pill first and then drink the bad water.

yehyeh—Chinese word for grandpop on your dad's side. He's fantastic!

Yikes! Turn the page (if you dare) for a sneak peek at Alvin's new and totally terrifying adventures in

ALVIN HO

ALLERGIC TO BIRTHDAY PARTIES, SCIENCE PROJECTS, AND OTHER MAN-MADE CATASTROPHES

A Two-Pound Hairball

TGIS. Thank God it was Saturday.

On Saturdays, I'm—FIRECRACKER MAN!!!

"Bakbakbakbakbakbak!" I screamed, popping like a string of firecrackers on Chinese New Year. I was zooming around my yard in my Firecracker Man outfit, saving the world and keeping an eye on Lucy and another eye on Anibelly, who was

digging holes in the yard with one of my carved sticks.

"Lalalalalalala," sang Anibelly, who sings whenever she's happy.

If there's anything I love about Anibelly, it's this—she's happy. When you hang out with her, you feel happy too. For a little sister, she's okay. But if there's anything I don't love about Anibelly, it's that she's a girl. And girls are annoying, as everyone knows. She's practically attached to me like a flower to a stem. And it's hard to get away from her when you're the stem. But today I had an idea.

"B-R-B!" I screamed, which is faster to say than Be Right Back! Then I zoomed off, across our neighbor's yard, through the gate and down the street toward the noise coming from Jules's house, which is on the way to everything.

Through the bushes I could see that the gang was there, and everyone was galloping wildly about, hollering war cries that sounded like they were coming right out of King Philip's War. In fact, it *was* King Philip's War! And

King Philip's War, as everyone knows, is the war between settlers and natives that nearly wiped out all of Massachusetts a hundred years before the American Revolution wiped out everyone else. So when the gang isn't playing the American Revolution, they're playing King Philip's War.

"*Wooofwoooooff,*" said Lucy, who had followed me. She slipped through a crack in the bushes and into Jules's yard. Lucy always says hello. She's very friendly. And when she's with me, people are friendly to me too. So I slipped through the bushes after her.

"Hey, Alvin!" said Jules.

I tipped my head to one side. That's "hey" in body language.

It's hard to tell if Jules is a boy or a girl, but it didn't matter on account of the fantastic war paint on his or her face! Nhia was wearing a tricorn hat, and Scooter and Sam had on pilgrim hats from last year's Thanksgiving Day parade. Eli was dressed as Abraham Lincoln, who had come to dinner once in Concord, Massachusetts, which is hard to spell. And Abe Lincoln, as everyone knows, can play settlers and Indians without dressing like one if he wants. Pinky, who is very bossy, was wearing a big feather on his head and a blanket around his shoulders. He was the Indian leader, King Philip.

"It's settlers against Indians," called Sam. "We're practicing for Hobson's party."

"You're going, aren't you?" asked Eli.

I shrugged.

"Didn't you get an invitation?" asked Jules.

What invitation?

"Maybe you weren't invited," said Pinky, who speaks for everyone on account of he's the leader of the gang. Besides, Hobson wasn't there.

I shrugged. I don't like birthday parties anyway. They're unpredictable; anything can happen. And you have to be on your

best behavior the *whole* time. But I did want to play King Philip's War. And I did want to be invited to something with the rest of the gang.

"Do you have settler gear?" Pinky asked.

I shook my head no.

"How 'bout Indian gear?"

I shook my head again.

"No wonder you haven't been invited," said Pinky. "No war paint, no moccasins, no fun. As for today . . . you can be a watcher."

"Al-vin's a wat-cher," he sang. "Al-vin's a wat-cher."

I didn't want to be a watcher. I wanted to play. But the trouble with Pinky is that he makes

all the rules. And usually Rule Number 1 is that
I'm not allowed to join in.

"Well, there's only one way to find out if
you're going to Hobson's party," said Sam, taking
something out of his pocket. It looked like a
hairball the size of a fist. Everyone stopped dead
in his tracks.

"Sure is ugly," whistled Scooter.

"What is it?" I asked.

"The eyeball of a woolly mammoth,"
said Sam. "It weighs two pounds."

Everyone gasped.

Sam collects things. Things you'd never laid
your eyes on before. Things you never knew ex-
isted. And you never know what's going to be in
Sam's pockets, especially on Saturdays.

"Where'd you get it?" asked Nhia.

"On vacation," said Sam. He paused. He
stroked the eyeball. Then in a hushed voice, he
added, "It knows everything. It can see the future."

Everyone leaned in for a closer look.

"Ask it if Alvin will get an invitation,"
said Eli.

"It can't do anything on an empty stomach," said Sam. "You gotta feed it candy first."

I didn't have any candy, but I had a piece of gum in my pocket. "Here," I said.

Sam popped the gum right into his mouth, chewed, then spat some of the juice into the woolly eye. "Will Alviiiiin get an iiiiiinviiiiiiitation to the paarty?" Sam asked the eye.

I held my breath.

There was no answer.

"It's crying for candy," said Sam.

Everyone could see that the eye was not crying. There were no tears. But everyone knew where there was a LOT of candy. Eli. Eli's pockets are practically a candy store. And his teeth are ugly to prove it.

So the gang jumped on Eli and cleaned out his pockets. And when it was all laid out on the grass, anyone could tell that there was enough candy to see one hundred years into the future!

After a couple of practice pieces, everyone stuffed their cheeks and got ready. Sam rubbed

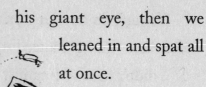

his giant eye, then we leaned in and spat all at once.

"Mammoth eye," said Sam, drooling heavily, "will Alviiiiin get an iiiiiiiiinviiiiiiiiitation?"

Suddenly, the eye started rolling in Sam's hands, slowly at first, then faster and faster! It was terrific! Then Sam dropped it. *Pllluuup!*

"Oops," slurped Sam.

Lucy raced up and put the eye on top of her paws and touched her nose to it in the downward-dog position. Lucy's an expert yoga baller. She can hold her pose until the mammoths thaw.

"What did it say?" I asked.

"It said YYYYYES!" said Sam.

Yes? I didn't hear anything.

"Are you sure?" I asked.

"No," said Sam. "But it'll take some more candy to make sure."

But there was no more candy. We'd eaten the whole store.

And the thing about candy is this. There's LOTS of sugar in it. And when you have that much sugar for breakfast, it makes you go fast-forward like a maniac for no reason at all and you can't stop or rewind.

"AAAAAAAAAAAAAAAAAAACK!" I screamed at the top of my lungs, running full speed ahead, clanging on my Firecracker Man helmet.

"AAAAAAAAAAAAAAAAAAAACK!" screamed the gang, ricocheting around the yard like loose pinballs. No one was playing settlers and Indians anymore, but it was okay. You can wear anything when it's not a war.

That night, after everyone had gone to bed and my brother Calvin was fast asleep, I was still wide awake thinking about what the mammoth eye had said.

YYYYYYES!

Yes meant I was going to get an invitation.

My eyes opened wide.

I popped out of bed and rushed over to the window. It was a clear and twinkly night. Up in the sky were so many stars, it looked like someone had spilled them, like Anibelly spilling all her jacks.

"I wish I may, I wish I might," I whispered against the cold glass, "have the first wish I wish upon a star tonight."

"*Grrrrrrrrrr,*" said Calvin. "*Grrrrrrrrrrrr.*"

Calvin's a sleep talker. There's no cure for it; it runs in my family. On days when he's done something bad, his entire criminal history will slip out like a greased bicycle chain, just like that.

I listened.

Nothing.

His blankets went up and down.

So I turned back to face the stars.

"I wish . . . ," I began, "I wish . . ."

There were LOTS of stars out, glittering like a million pieces of glass in the street. I could see the Big Dipper and, right above it, the North Star.

"I wish for the deluxe Indian Chief outfit with fringe," I said, my breath dripping on the glass. "Complete with bow and arrow and the huge feather headdress that makes you look like a giant bird."

I crossed my fingers. It was a big wish. I'd wished for the deluxe Indian Chief outfit every Christmas and never gotten it. How was I going to get my hands on it now, just so Hobson would invite me to his party?

I didn't know.

"I love you, stars," I added, just in case.

Then I ran and jumped into bed before the flesh-eating critters under my bed could grab me.